"You're jumping to conclusions, Joni," said Crystal. "Have you actually *seen* Beau flirting with anyone?"

"Well," Joni said, "I'm going to leave my own message on Boy Talk. I'm going to tell Sneaking Around off big time and order her to leave my boyfriend *alone!*"

"You can't do that!" shrieked Su-Su, throwing herself across the answering machine. "You don't know who Sneaking Around is! You don't even know if Beau is the boy she's talking about. There are almost eight hundred kids in our school. It could be *anybody.*"

For a moment, Joni didn't answer. A picture of Beau strolling into the movie theater with another girl flashed into her mind. Tears filled her eyes.

How dare Beau Maguire sneak around and take out someone behind my back? she thought.

#1
SNEAKING AROUND

by Betsy Haynes

BULLSEYE BOOKS

Random House   New York

For Mae Sheridan, with sincere affection

A BULLSEYE BOOK PUBLISHED BY RANDOM HOUSE, INC.

Copyright © 1995 by Betsy Haynes. Cover art copyright © 1995 by Aleta Jenks. All rights reserved under International and Pan-American Copyright Conventions. Published in the United States by Random House, Inc., New York, and simultaneously in Canada by Random House of Canada Limited, Toronto.

Library of Congress Catalog Card Number: 94-067695
ISBN: 0-679-86022-3
RL: 5.0

Manufactured in the United States of America   10 9 8 7 6 5 4 3 2 1

BOY TALK™ is a trademark of Random House, Inc., and Betsy Haynes

Chapter One

Joni Sparkman opened her locker and darted a quick look into the mirror hanging inside the door. She poked at her bangs a couple of times so that anyone looking her way would think she was just fixing her short, dark hair. Actually she was checking out the scene behind her.

April Mathis was making her way along the locker-lined hallway. Naturally Molly Triola and Kristin Murphy were with her. They followed April everywhere. They even tried to dress like her. Joni thought it was disgusting.

But lots of girls worshiped April. She was captain of the cheerleading squad and the most popular girl in the seventh grade at Sunshine Beach Middle School in Sunshine Beach, Florida.

Joni watched April move from locker to locker, stopping at some and going right on past others. Each time she stopped, there was a flurry of excitement as she handed a small white envelope to the boy or girl standing there. Then she would flash a big smile and move on, coming closer and closer to Joni.

"I don't care if I get invited to her pool party or not," Joni muttered to herself.

Still, the word around school was that Saturday night's party was going to be huge. Joni hated the thought of being one of the few left out. And she couldn't resist watching April, with her violet eyes and shoulder-length brown hair that always looked so perfect.

Joni raked her fingers through her own hair. It never looked perfect. Most of the time it looked as windblown as when she rode her jet ski at the beach. She couldn't care less. She liked her own hair just fine, thank you.

April Mathis would probably grow up to be a movie star or a model. But what Joni wanted to be was a mystery writer. She devoured mysteries at the rate of two or three a week, especially those in the Lindsey Jones mystery series. Right now Joni was trying out the mirror trick Lindsey used in *The Valentine Corpse* to spy on April passing out her invitations.

Classes had been dismissed for the day several minutes ago. The crowd that had been pushing and shoving and yelling and banging locker doors was getting smaller and quieter. Joni held her breath as April stopped at the locker next to hers and handed Marissa Pauley an envelope.

"Hope you can come," Joni heard April say cheerily. Then she breezed past Joni without so much as a glance in her direction.

Joni stared into her locker for a moment, letting the idea sink in that she was definitely being excluded from April's party. Sighing, she slammed the locker door and hurried off to meet her two best friends.

Crystal Britton and Su-Su McCarthy were waiting for her by the front door. Crystal sat on the steps, and Su-Su leaned against the building, fanning herself with a floppy denim hat.

"Oh, there you are," said Crystal, looking up. She gave Joni a big smile, and a dimple appeared in her left cheek like magic.

"Where have you been?" asked Su-Su. "The bell rang ages ago."

"Watching April Mathis pass out her party invitations," Joni said, sighing.

"Did you get one?" asked Su-Su eagerly as the three of them started down the sidewalk.

Joni shook her head. "How about you guys?"

"Nope," said Su-Su, twirling a lock of red hair around a finger. "But it doesn't surprise me. This morning my horoscope said 'Someone's grudge from the past will return to affect your future.' Remember last week in the cafeteria when April gave us that incredibly dirty look because she thought we were talking about her?"

"That's so unfair. We *weren't* talking about her, remember?" Crystal protested, sounding hurt. "I was going on and on about Evan Byrnes and how I keep wishing he'd break up with Alison Hamel so I could have a chance with him."

Joni shrugged. "Maybe April wants to be able to gossip about us at her party."

"Gossip about us? Get serious," scoffed Su-Su. "We never do anything worth gossiping about. Except—" she raised an eyebrow and grinned at Joni—maybe you, Joni. You're the one with a boyfriend."

"Forget it," said Joni. "Beau and I have never done anything we couldn't put in the school paper."

She started down the sidewalk, thinking that she really didn't need April and her crowd. She had the two best friends on earth. Crystal, with her curly, honey-colored hair and dimple, was only four feet eleven inches tall, but she had an enormous heart. In fact, she was one of the sweetest, most caring people Joni had ever known. She was always there when anyone had a problem or needed a shoulder to cry on.

Su-Su McCarthy, whose full name was Susan Suzanna McCarthy, was named for her two grand-mothers and nicknamed Su-Su when she was a baby. Su-Su was the tallest girl in their class, and with her flaming red hair, she was easy to spot in a crowd. She was a natural comedienne who loved to wear bizarre clothes and entertain her friends with dramatic sto-ries. She planned her entire life around her daily horoscope.

"I heard that April is inviting tons of boys," said Crystal, breaking into Joni's thoughts. "The only rea-son I want to go is because Evan will probably be there. Did Beau get an invitation?"

The question startled Joni. "Gosh, I don't know," she said. "April wouldn't do something that sneaky, would she? I mean, she knows he's my boyfriend."

"Are you kidding?" asked Su-Su. "April does any-thing she feels like doing. And she wouldn't miss a chance to invite a guy as popular as Beau Maguire to her party."

Joni frowned. "Right," she mumbled. She had to talk to Beau—soon.

As if on cue, she heard someone yelling her name. "Hey, Joni! Wait up!"

She looked around to see Beau hurrying up the sidewalk behind her, his pale blond hair shining in the sunlight. He looked so handsome it almost took her breath away. Today he was wearing one of her favorite outfits, faded jeans and a denim vest that showed off his super build.

Her happiness lasted only a split second. Beau's three best buddies were loping up the sidewalk beside him. Dan Turpin, tall and skinny as a palm tree, was nicknamed Twister because he was constantly in motion, like a tornado. Parker Hatch was Twister's opposite, short and stocky. Joni thought he had a laugh like a hyena. Jason Duffy's huge glasses gave him a geeky look, but he was hardly a world-class brain. Just like the other two, Jason was loud and obnoxious. To make matters worse, Beau had a bad habit of acting just like them when they were all together.

To her dismay, Joni saw that Beau was grinning like crazy and waving a small white envelope in the air.

"We all got invited to April Mathis's pool party Saturday night," he said excitedly. "You're going, aren't you?"

Joni exchanged embarrassed glances with Crystal and Su-Su and shook her head.

Beau looked surprised. "You mean she didn't invite you guys? I wonder why."

Before Joni could think up an answer, Twister guffawed. "Aw, poor Schwartzy. He's going to have to go to the party without his lover girl." He wrapped his arms around himself and kissed the air so dramatically that the red-and-white bandanna tied over his short brown hair slipped down on his forehead.

"Schwartzy can go without you, can't he, Joni?" asked Parker, grinning wickedly. He got down on one knee and held clasped hands out toward her. "Please say he can. Pretty please."

Joni saw Beau's face turning red. She hated it when his friends teased him about her. She couldn't stand their nickname for him: Schwartzy, which was short for Arnold Schwarzenegger. Beau had the best build of any boy in seventh grade.

"Don't worry, Joni. We'll fill you in on all the girls Beau kisses underwater," said Jason, laughing. He poked Beau in the ribs with his elbow. "Hey, do you think April will wear a bikini? Wow!"

"You guys are so *gross!*" Su-Su said angrily.

Crystal tugged on Joni's sleeve. "Come on, Joni, let's get out of here."

Part of Joni wanted to stick her nose in the air and stomp away with her two best friends. She was dying to show Beau how angry she was at his friends, but she couldn't. Not when he was about to tell her that he liked her too much to go to April's party without her.

Beau shifted from one foot to the other and glanced at his friends. They were looking back at him expectantly with cocky grins on their faces.

Giving Joni a sheepish look, he said, "Hey, it sounds like a great party. Too bad you aren't going, but we'll tell you all about it afterwards. Right, guys?"

Joni felt the fury building inside her like an erupting volcano. "Beau Maguire! How can you go to that party when I'm not invited?"

Beau looked uncertain for a moment. Then he straightened his broad shoulders and flashed Joni an angry look. "It's no big deal," he said.

Behind him, Parker, Jason, and Twister snickered. "Beau Maguire, how *dare* you go to the party without me!" Parker mimicked in an extra-high voice.

"Hey, Schwartzy, how does it feel to have a *girl* running your life?" teased Twister.

"Nobody's running my life," Beau muttered. "Come on. Let's go shoot some hoops."

A huge lump filled Joni's throat as Beau and his friends turned away and headed down the street.

Chapter Two

Joni looked at her watch for the hundredth time in the past hour. It was Saturday night, and April's party had started fifty-seven minutes ago. Joni, Su-Su, and Crystal were sitting around in Crystal's bedroom, listening to CDs. They had decided to have a slumber party to keep their minds off the pool party, but so far the atmosphere was pretty gloomy.

"I wonder what's going on at April's right now," Joni said glumly. "Do you think they're all in the pool?"

Crystal shrugged. "I'll bet they're having a better time than we are. Let's face it, this is almost as much fun as getting a tetanus shot."

"I'm so bored I'm going to count my freckles for

excitement," mumbled Su-Su. "Where's your mirror, Crystal?"

Joni was sprawled across the floor on her back, staring at the ceiling. She couldn't stop thinking about Beau. Was he flirting with cute girls in bikinis? Maybe even kissing someone underwater, like Jason had said?

The truth was, she was beginning to think she didn't know Beau nearly as well as she'd thought.

A few months ago, she'd had a hard time believing that someone as popular as Beau Maguire would be interested in her. After all, he was a major hunk and captain of the wrestling team.

It had all started one Sunday at the beach, with her parents and Hannah, her six-year-old sister. All she'd wanted to do was stretch out in the warm sun in her bikini and read a Lindsey Jones novel in peace. Then her parents asked her to watch Hannah while they walked up the beach. And that was the moment when Hannah turned into a pain.

"I'm going into the water," she announced as soon as their parents were out of earshot.

"Hannah, you know you can't go in by yourself," Joni had said, giving her little sister an annoyed look.

"You can go in with me," Hannah said in a sugary voice. "You're not doing anything."

Joni snorted in exasperation. "Not doing anything! I'm reading and catching a few rays. Mom and Dad will be back in a little while. They'll take you in."

"But I want to go in the water now," Hannah insisted. She stuck out her lower lip in a pout. "*Please*, Joni."

Hannah kept on begging until Joni gave up trying to reason with her and started to ignore her. Suddenly Hannah grabbed two handfuls of sand and threw them on Joni's nearly bare back.

Joni let out a shriek and jumped to her feet.

"Now you *have* to go into the water to wash off," Hannah said gleefully.

Joni tried to brush off the sand, but she had put on so much sunscreen that most of the sand was stuck to her skin. "Hannah Sparkman, I'm going to murder you!" she shouted and lunged toward her little sister.

Hannah ducked away. Just as Joni started after her, she heard someone else yell, "Hey, kid! Want to see a sea monster?"

To Joni's surprise, Beau Maguire was kneeling in the sand only ten feet away. The sun had bleached his blond hair almost white, playing up his deep tan. Beside him was a half-finished sand sculpture of a sea monster with a long snout and spiked tail.

"I could sure use some help finishing this," he said to Hannah. Then he shot a laser-beam smile straight at Joni.

Her heart did a triple flip as she smiled back. Not

only had he rescued her from murdering her little sister, but it looked as if he had done it on purpose!

Hannah helped Beau finish the sea monster, and so did Joni. Then Beau and Joni took Hannah into the water for a swim. By the time her parents returned, Beau had asked Joni for their very first date. That was six months ago, and they had been together almost every weekend since then. Until now...

"Earth to Sparkman," Su-Su said, breaking into Joni's thoughts. "What are you thinking about?"

Joni sighed. "That day at the beach when Beau asked me out for the first time."

"Oh, yeah," Crystal said in a dreamy voice. "I remember that. Beau is so romantic."

"*Except* when he's with his friends," snapped Joni. "They're stupid jerks, and when he's with them, he acts like a stupid jerk, too. You saw him the other day when he got the invitation to April's party. He acted as if going along with the guys was a lot more important than hurting me."

"Boys are so insensitive sometimes," said Su-Su.

"And so immature," added Crystal.

Joni felt a rush of gratitude for her two best friends. They were trying so hard to make her feel better. "Thanks, guys," she said. "I just wish we'd gotten invited to April's party, too. Then I wouldn't be making you both so miserable by moping around over Beau."

"What's wrong with us?" Su-Su said with a sigh. She was sitting cross-legged on the floor beside the CD player. Ten bottles of fingernail polish were lined up in front of her, and she was laboriously applying a different color of polish on each nail. "Practically everybody in our class was invited," she added, blowing on her wet nails.

"Tell me about it," Joni muttered. "They're probably all having a great time, too."

"Not *everybody* got invited," Crystal pointed out. "I know lots of kids who didn't. Shauna Roberts is really popular. She sits next to me in English, and she didn't get an invitation. Neither did any of her friends."

"Did Evan and Alison get invited?" asked Su-Su. Evan was Crystal's next-door neighbor.

"Naturally," Crystal replied sadly. "Have you noticed how Alison treats him like dirt? I would be *sooo* sweet to him."

"How come all the cute guys are always taken?" Su-Su grumbled. "Why can't I find one?"

"You will," Crystal said sympathetically.

Joni was staring out the window, thinking about Beau again. "Guys, I need to talk to you about something," she said suddenly. "But you've got to *promise* you won't tell *anybody*." She looked at Su-Su and then at Crystal, who was sitting on her bed, thumbing through a magazine.

"You can trust us," said Crystal. "We're your best friends."

"I know," said Joni. "It's just that for the past couple of weeks I've had this feeling that Beau doesn't like me anymore."

"You're kidding," said Su-Su, looking surprised. "I thought you guys were really close."

"We are," said Joni. "At least we *were*," she corrected. "He used to call me every day after school, and we'd talk for practically forever. He'd ask me lots of things, like what my favorite pizza is and what bands I like. We had tons of things in common."

"So what happened?" asked Crystal.

"I don't know. Things seemed to be going great, but ..." Joni searched for words. "It's just *different* now. He hardly ever calls, and he doesn't talk to me at school much anymore, either. He's always hanging out with his friends. I think he's avoiding me. I just wish I knew why, and what I could do about it."

"Come on, Joni," Su-Su said, "your imagination's getting out of hand again. It's all those mysteries you keep reading. They make you suspicious of things that are perfectly normal."

"But, Su-Su," Joni insisted, "you don't understand. Beau *is* acting different."

"Maybe you should read your horoscope," said Su-Su. Her face brightened. "You're a Scorpio, right?

Let's find today's paper and see what it says."

Su-Su was scrambling to her feet when Crystal cried excitedly, "Hey, look at this!" She pointed to an advertisement in the back of the teen magazine she had been thumbing through. "I've just found the answer to our problems."

"What is it?" asked Su-Su, craning her neck to see.

"It's called Romance Rap," said Crystal. "It's a 900 telephone number you can call to talk about your problems. Here, listen to this."

A big smile crossed her face as she began reading out loud, "'Romance! Dating! Friendship! Talk to teens all over the country. Ask for advice on your boy problems. Be a best friend and help someone else. All you need is a Touch-Tone phone A dollar ninety-five per minute. Under eighteen ask permis sion before calling.' Doesn't that sound cool? Joni, you ought to call and ask for advice about Beau. I might even ask how to tear Evan away from Alison."

"Incredible! Maybe *I* could find out how to attract guys! Give me that magazine," said Su-Su. She quickly scanned the ad, then handed the magazine to Joni.

"Let's do it!" Joni cried.

Crystal scrambled off the bed. "Let's call from my dad's office. We can all listen in on his speaker-phone."

Joni and Su-Su followed her across the hall and

into the book-lined bedroom that Mr. Britton had converted into an office. He worked there every morning, writing a syndicated newspaper column. Afternoons he taught political science at the local college.

It was the first time Joni had ever been in Mr. Britton's office. Dozens of framed awards hung on one wall. Her gaze swept the big oak desk beside the window. On it were a messy stack of papers, ball-point pens, a calendar, and a family picture of Crystal and her mom and dad taken a few months before Mrs. Britton died when Crystal was six. But the thing that really caught Joni's eye was the huge telephone in the center of the desk. Beside it was the most elaborate answering machine she had ever seen. It had at least a dozen buttons on top.

Crystal took the magazine over to the desk. She hit the speaker button and they heard a loud dial tone. Carefully she punched in the Romance Rap number.

"Everybody ready?" she asked, grinning. Joni could hear the telephone ringing on the other end.

After two rings a girl's perky voice said, "Hello, and welcome to Romance Rap! I'm so glad you called. In just a few moments, you're going to get the chance to share secrets with girls just like yourself and get advice for your problems from teens all over the country. You'll love Romance Rap so much that you'll want to call over and over again. Listen closely, and I'll tell you how it works."

"Oh, my gosh!" whispered Joni.

Su-Su started snapping her fingers and moving to the beat of the recorded music. "Gotta listen 'cause it's cool. Got our-selves a ro-mance school," she sang, making up the words as she went along.

Crystal and Joni giggled at Su-Su, and the three of them gathered around the desk as the instructions continued. "If you want to *ask* advice for your problem, punch one after the beep and record your message. Then call back tomorrow and hear all the messages for you.

"If you want to *give* advice for someone else's problem, punch two to record your message. And if you just want to listen in, punch three to hear problems other girls have recorded or four to hear advice that new friends from all over the country have offered. If at any time you want to change, just push the number of your new choice. Thanks again for calling!" The instant the girl stopped talking, loud music began blasting over the line.

"Let's listen to problems first," Joni suggested.

Su-Su nodded, and Crystal pushed on the keypad.

Joni held her breath. If she was lucky, someone else might call in with a problem like hers. Then she'd be able to get some quick advice without actually having to talk.

"Hello, Romance Rap?" said a nervous-sounding girl. "This is Ignored, and I live in Phoenix. I have this really major problem with a boy I like. He tells all my friends that he likes me, but he never asks me out. He even calls my friends on the phone to talk to them about me. I'd give anything if he'd call me instead. What can I do to get him to show me that he likes me? I really hope you can help."

Joni, Crystal, and Su-Su sat glued to the phone as it beeped again and another voice came on.

"Hi." There was a long silence. "Is anybody there? I mean, I've never done anything like this before, and it feels really weird." There was another long silence. "Well, anyway, here goes. This is Confused in Virginia. I like this incredible guy, and he likes me. The one problem is, he's sixteen and has his driver's license, and I'm only thirteen. Everybody says he's too old for me, but I don't think so. I mean, he is *so* cool. Not like the dweebs in my grade. Anyway, I need to know what everyone else thinks before I tell my parents about him. Um … bye."

"Go on, Joni, ask for advice about Beau," urged Su-Su. "It's your big chance."

Joni bit her lower lip and stared at the phone. Now she could understand why Confused in Virginia had been so nervous. It was scary to think that girls all over the country were listening. "Maybe later," she told her friends. "I … I want to listen more first."

"Chicken!" teased Su-Su.

Crystal pressed 4 to listen to advice that had been recorded for earlier problems. They heard Big Sis in Baltimore tell Chained to a Jerk in Des Moines that she thought the best way to break up with a boy she didn't like anymore was to level with him about the romance part of their relationship and ask if they could still be friends.

Joni sighed. So far no one had mentioned a problem like hers. After a dozen more calls, she glanced at her watch and gasped.

"Yikes!" she cried. "We've been listening for thirty-seven minutes! That'll cost us ... um ... thirty-seven minutes times a dollar ninety-five per minute ..."

Crystal pounded numbers into a calculator lying on her father's desk. "Seventy-two dollars and fifteen cents!" she shrieked and hurriedly hung up the phone. "My dad's going to *kill* me!"

Joni looked at her friends in horror, doing calculations in her head. "That comes out to twenty-four dollars and five cents—*apiece*! Where are we going to get that kind of money?"

Two pairs of eyes stared back at her. No one said a word.

Chapter Three

Joni, Crystal, and Su-Su sat up half the night talking about Romance Rap. They slept in until eleven-thirty the next morning.

"I'm dying to find out what went on at April's party," said Joni. They were sitting around the breakfast table in their bathrobes, eating cold pizza left over from the night before.

Su-Su wiped a blob of tomato sauce off her sleep shirt. "You could call Beau," she said. "Just kidding," she added quickly when Joni frowned at her.

Crystal brightened. "I know. Why don't we go to the beach? We could work on our tans and see if anybody's there who went to the party last night."

"Nah," said Joni. "After that pool party last night,

I'll bet nobody will be at the beach today."

"Okay then, how about the mall?" offered Crystal.

"Good idea," said Joni.

The girls dressed quickly and rode their bikes to Royal Palms Mall, which was about two miles from Crystal's house. The huge, sprawling building was painted flamingo pink with a white tile roof. It had an open-air food court in the center. The girls locked up their bikes at a rack near the main entrance and went inside.

"I just can't stop thinking about Romance Rap," Su-Su said as they sauntered along, gazing in store windows and keeping an eye out for anyone they knew.

"Me neither," said Crystal. "Especially when I picture my dad opening the next phone bill. I actually had a nightmare about it last night. He went berserk and came after me like this." She held out her arms and started walking stiff-legged like Frankenstein, a wild look in her eyes.

Su-Su and Joni broke up laughing.

"Don't worry," said Joni. "We'll pay him back just as soon as we can. I can baby-sit to earn my part of the money."

"Me, too. I just wish calling Romance Rap wasn't so expensive," said Su-Su. "I could really use some advice on becoming a guy magnet." She stopped in front of a store window and struck a glamorous pose. "How's this?"

Joni rolled her eyes. "You *do* need help."

"I know what you mean, Su-Su," said Crystal. "Just think how great it would be to talk to all those other girls about things that are really important and really private. Girls besides just us, who have had more experience with boys."

"Exactly," said Su-Su. "People who couldn't blab our personal business all over school."

"Well we might as well forget Romance Rap," Joni said dejectedly. "We won't be able to afford another call before the year 2010!"

They wandered into Pet Me!, the mall's pet shop. Crystal instantly began cooing to a tiny white Lhasa apso puppy in a cage. Su-Su played with a gray and white kitten.

Joni stared absently at the cages of animals lining the walls. Normally she loved to come to Pet Me! and see the adorable puppies and kittens, but today she couldn't think of anything but Romance Rap. She needed some anonymous advice a lot more than either of her friends did. It had been two weeks since she and Beau had last gone out. She really was beginning to believe he liked someone else. After all, it wasn't like he had to get up the nerve to tell her or anything.

Should she ask him about it? What if he admitted

he liked somebody else and then told her to get lost? She would absolutely die. *There has to be a better way to find out what's going on with Beau,* she thought.

Suddenly, just as they were heading back into the mall, an idea popped into Joni's mind. She stopped in her tracks, causing Crystal, who was walking behind her, to bump into her.

"Whoa, guys!" Joni said breathlessly as the crowd of shoppers swirled around them. "Want to hear something that's really brilliant? I mean *seriously* brilliant!"

Crystal and Su-Su blinked at her in surprise. "Sure," said Su-Su. "Fire away."

"I honestly think we could do it!" Joni said excitedly. "And it would be incredible! It would solve all of our problems!" The words were tumbling out faster than she could control them.

"What are you *talking* about?" asked Su-Su, rolling her eyes.

Just then a little boy about two years old pulled away from his mother and crashed into Joni's knees. His frazzled mother, who was also pushing a baby in a stroller, mumbled an apology and grabbed the toddler's hand again.

"Let's sit over there, guys," Joni said. She motioned toward an empty bench beside a pool with huge goldfish swimming in it.

Joni started talking again before Crystal and Su-Su

had even sat down. "We could use your father's answering machine after school while he's at the college, Crystal! Don't you see? That way, nobody would ever figure out it was us."

"My dad's answering machine?" Crystal looked puzzled. "I think you're losing it, Joni."

"Yeah," said Su-Su. "You're not making any sense."

"Okay, okay." Joni waved them away. She leaned close to her friends and tried to slow down. "Listen to this. We can start our *own* Romance Rap! How's that for an awesome idea?"

For a split second, Crystal and Su-Su looked bewildered. Then big grins spread slowly across their faces.

"Yeah! It's an *incredibly* awesome idea!" cried Crystal. "My dad has a separate telephone number for his office. It's even unlisted. We could give out that number and tell kids to call after school, while he's at work. They could record messages on my dad's phone the same way they do on Romance Rap."

"Exactly," said Joni. "And we could put a greeting at the beginning of the tape telling everyone what to do, just like the one we heard on Romance Rap. Isn't there a number to punch in after the greeting if you want to listen to the messages already recorded on the tape?"

Crystal nodded. "I've seen my dad do that when

we've been out of town visiting my Aunt Susan. It's easy." She thought a minute and frowned. "Big problem. If we record our message over my dad's, how do we put it back when we're finished?"

Nobody said anything for a minute. Then Joni had another idea. "I've got a tape recorder. We can tape your dad's message before we put our own on and then re-record his message when we're finished."

"That's brilliant," said Su-Su.

"Hey, wait a minute," said Crystal. "Here's another problem. What if someone recognizes our voices? They'd know it was us."

"Let me handle that," said Su-Su. "Have you forgotten that I am the world's greatest actress?" She pulled herself up to her fullest height and gave them a superior smile. "I will simply disguise my voice."

"Wow! This is sounding better all the time," said Crystal. "Why don't we make flyers and leave them around school?"

"Great," said Joni. "Now all we have to do is think of a cool name. We can't use Romance Rap. That's already taken."

"I think the title should have the word 'boys' in it," Crystal said. "That's most girls' favorite subject."

"Tell me about it," said Su-Su. "I'd rather talk about boys than anything else in the world."

"That's it!" cried Joni. "Boy Talk! It's the perfect name."

Su-Su punched the air with her fist. "Yes!" she yelled triumphantly. Several shoppers passing by turned to stare at her.

Crystal didn't say anything. She was looking worried again. "Wait a minute, guys," she said. "What if my dad finds out about Boy Talk? I'll be in enough trouble when he gets that phone bill. I don't know what he'd do if he found out we were using his business phone number for a teen advice hot line. Ground me until I'm twenty-one, probably."

"Crystal, there's nothing to worry about," Joni assured her. "He'll never find out. We'll make sure kids know that they can only call after school. We can put the times to call in the flyer. Your dad won't suspect a thing. By the time he gets home, his own tape will be safely back in the machine."

"Okay," Crystal said, still sounding a little reluctant. "If you say so."

Su-Su took her by the arm. "Come on. Let's go to the food court and find a table. We've got some serious planning to do."

Chapter Four

"I need fries," Su-Su announced as they walked into the food court. "I can't think on an empty stomach."

"Me neither," Joni agreed.

A few minutes later, the three girls were seated at a table, munching french fries and sipping sodas as they discussed Boy Talk.

"I'm definitely going to ask for some advice," said Su-Su. "Do you guys realize that no matter what I do, cute boys never notice me? It's the pits."

"Get serious, Su-Su," Joni said. "How could anybody help but notice you? You're taaaall, thiiiin, goooorgeous, and a person practically has to wear sunglasses to look at your hair. Besides, look at the kind of clothes you wear. Anybody would have to be blind not to notice you."

Su-Su glanced across the table at Joni and Crystal, who were both wearing shorts and tank tops, and then down at her own World War II-style military jacket and tall lace-up boots. "I still need help," she said, shrugging.

"I feel like 'Dear Abby' already," Crystal said. "I can't *wait* for kids to start calling."

"Imagine all the secrets we're going to hear," said Su-Su. She rubbed her hands together in anticipation. "Besides getting advice for our own problems, we'll be able to listen in on the private lives of everyone at school!"

"Gosh, I hadn't thought about that," said Crystal. "This is getting better by the minute."

"Wouldn't it be a riot if April Mathis called in with a big romance problem?" Su-Su asked.

"That'll be the day," Joni grumbled. "I can't imagine April having a problem with anything." She began fuming again at the thought of Beau at April's pool party the night before.

"Do you really think kids will call in?" asked Crystal. "Won't they figure out that someone from school is behind it?"

"Not if we make our flyers look totally professional," said Su-Su, dragging a french fry through a blob of ketchup. "We can't just scribble something on a sheet of paper with a Magic Marker."

"I guess it would be too expensive to run an ad in the newspaper," said Crystal with a sigh. "Especially since we owe so much on the phone bill."

"I know," Joni piped up. "Why don't we use your dad's computer, Crystal? I've seen some of the school projects you've done on it. They looked awfully professional to me."

"Eeek!" Crystal squealed. "Why do *I* have to take all the chances? I'll have to sneak around to use it. What if Dad finds out what I'm doing?"

"Chill out," said Su-Su. "You can pretend you're doing homework. Besides, it's for a good cause—*us.* Don't you want to find out how to rescue Evan Byrnes from Alison Hamel's greedy clutches?"

Crystal gave her a big grin. "You're right. I can't wait!"

"Can't wait for what?"

Joni looked up to see Beau and Parker Hatch standing beside their table. Beau had his baseball cap on backward and was giving her a cocky smile. Parker looked as gross as ever. He was eating a triple chocolate ice cream cone that was dripping down his arm onto his shirt.

Joni felt her face turn red. *Could they possibly have heard what we were talking about?* she thought with alarm.

"Oh, nothing," she said, trying to sound casual.

"Yeah, right," said Beau. "I guess since they won't tell us, it must be pretty interesting. Right, Hatchet Man?"

Parker nodded. "Maybe we'd better stick around for a while, just in case they decide to tell us."

"Good idea," said Beau. He dragged up a chair from an empty table and dropped down in it. Then he folded his arms, looking as if he were prepared to stay for a while.

"Hey, you girls missed a great party last night," said Parker in a cocky voice. "It was amazing, wasn't it, Schwartzy?"

Beau shrugged. "Yeah, I guess as parties go, it wasn't bad."

"You mean you actually went?" Joni asked angrily. She hadn't really believed that he'd stay home just because she couldn't go—not after the way he'd been acting lately. But it made her furious to hear him bragging about it in front of everyone anyway.

Beau looked uncomfortable and didn't answer. "Sure he went," said Parker. "It wasn't his fault you didn't get an invitation. Anyway, we swam awhile in April's huge pool and then went into the rec room. April kept the lights real low, and her parents stayed out of sight. Not bad, huh, Schwartzy?"

Beau nodded. "The food was great. They ordered a ton of pizzas." He stood up and nodded to Parker. "Come on, let's hit the arcade." Then, glancing back at Joni, he added, "See you around."

Tears welled up in Joni's eyes as she watched Beau and Parker walk away. *How can he act like this is no big deal?* she wondered miserably. *Can't he see how much it hurts me?*

"Boy Talk can't get started fast enough to suit me," she told her friends. "I really need advice badly. Beau makes me so confused." She shook her head in frustration.

"He actually seemed a little embarrassed about going to the party," said Crystal. "Isn't that a pretty good sign that he still likes you?"

"Who knows?" mumbled Joni. "I'm not sure if it means he's sorry he went to the party without me, or he flirted with somebody behind my back and now he's feeling guilty."

Crystal gave Joni a sympathetic look. "Guys can be such a pain sometimes."

"Yeah," Joni said, standing up from the table and gathering up her empty soda cup and greasy french fry container. "Let's go. We can stop by my house to get my tape recorder on the way to Crystal's house. If we work fast, we'll be able to start Boy Talk *tomorrow.*"

It was almost dark when Joni left Crystal's house and headed for home on her bicycle. Everything was ready for Boy Talk to start the next afternoon.

Mr. Britton had been watching a football game on TV in the family room while she, Crystal, and Su-Su had printed a fantastic flyer upstairs on his computer and made copies on his copy machine. Joni had designed the flyers herself, and she was very proud of them.

♡ ♡ ♡ ♡ ♡ ♡ ♡ ♡ ♡ ♡ ♡ ♡ ♡ ♡ ♡ ♡

BOY TALK

♡ *Totally confidential! Absolutely free!*
♡ *Romance! Dating! Friendship!*
♡ *Share your secrets with other teens!*
♡ *Ask for help with your boyfriend problems!*
♡ *Give advice and be a best friend to someone else!*

CALL 555-3902

After school Monday–Friday, 3:30–4:30

♡ ♡ ♡ ♡ ♡ ♡ ♡ ♡ ♡ ♡ ♡ ♡ ♡ ♡ ♡ ♡

She was humming to herself when she rode up the driveway. Suddenly she skidded to a stop. Beau was sitting on the front step.

"Where have you been?" he asked when she parked her bike and walked toward him. "I was just about to give up and go home."

"I was at Crystal's," said Joni. Her heart was thudding in her chest. She didn't know whether to be glad to see him or worried. Why was Beau here? To break up with her?

"Do you want to come in?" she asked.

"Sure," he said. He stood up and followed her inside.

Mr. and Mrs. Sparkman were sitting at the kitchen table, playing Pictionary with Hannah. They smiled and said hello.

Hannah looked up and blinked at Beau in surprise. "You're still here? I thought you went home ages ago."

Beau flushed. "I . . . I just needed to ask Joni something . . . about our homework assignment," he said, fumbling the words.

Joni smiled to herself. *Maybe he isn't here to break up after all*, she thought.

"Want to go out onto the patio?" she asked.

Beau nodded.

Joni knew that Hannah was watching them suspiciously as they walked through the open sliding glass doors and out to the screen-enclosed patio. Her little sister loved to spy on them. Once Hannah had even told their parents that Beau was holding Joni's hand while they watched television.

Stepping out into the twilight, Beau started talking before Joni had even had a chance to close the door behind them.

"I'm really sorry about April's party," he said. "I didn't want to go—not when I found out you weren't invited."

"Well, nobody forced you, did they?"

Beau fidgeted and looked down at his feet. "Not exactly. I mean, nobody *forced* me, but my friends sort of talked me into it. Don't worry. The party wasn't that great. Not as good as Parker made it sound today at the mall, anyway."

"Are you sure?" Joni pressed.

Beau nodded. "I wish you wouldn't be mad at me."

Joni didn't say anything for a moment. Beau was saying all the right things, but there was one thing that still bothered her.

"Why do you have to act like your friends when they're being obnoxious?" she asked.

Beau shrugged and looked away, but the next thing she knew, he had pulled her toward him and was kissing her. All of Joni's doubts suddenly faded away.

"I still like you. Honest," he said softly. "Do you believe me?"

Joni nodded, almost bursting with happiness. She had been so afraid that she was losing Beau, and now he had finally said the one thing she had wanted most to hear.

Her lips were still tingling from his kiss. "Do you

know what?" she blurted suddenly. Then she felt embarrassed and said shyly, "I guess I probably shouldn't tell you this."

"Tell me what?" he asked.

Joni hesitated. "I really shouldn't. I mean ... "

"Come on, tell me," Beau urged. "I don't care what it is."

"Oh, okay. The guys may call you Schwartzy, but I have a better nickname for you."

"What's that?" he asked.

"The World's Best Kisser," she said quickly before she could lose her nerve.

A smile lit up Beau's face, and he looked deep into her eyes. "That's *really* cool."

Then he started bouncing nervously from foot to foot. "Well, I gotta go," he said finally. "See ya."

He pushed through the screen door leading to the back yard and disappeared into the night.

"See ya," Joni told him softly. She drifted back into the house, floating three feet off the ground.

Chapter Five

Beau's kiss was the first thing that popped into Joni's mind when she opened her eyes the next morning.

"The World's Best Kisser," she whispered to herself and threw her pillow over her head. "I can't believe I actually *told* him that." But it was true.

She wanted to snuggle under the covers and dream about that kiss for a long, long time, but then she remembered why her alarm clock had gone off so early. She was supposed to meet Crystal and Su-Su at school forty-five minutes before the bell so they could leave Boy Talk flyers all over the building before any other kids began arriving.

She started to fling the covers aside and stopped, her arm suspended in midair. Suddenly Boy Talk didn't seem as important as it had before—not since last night and Beau's incredible kiss. Maybe she wouldn't even need Boy Talk now. But the thought of all her classmates' problems she would hear on Boy Talk propelled her out of bed.

When she ran across the school grounds a half an hour later, Crystal and Su-Su were sitting on the front steps. The two of them were looking around nervously as if they expected someone to appear and question them about being at school so early. Su-Su had pulled down the brim of her floppy denim hat to hide her face, but the flaming red hair that stuck out beneath it was a dead giveaway to her identity. Crystal was holding her math book up so that only her eyes showed above it.

"Sorry I'm late, but wait until I tell you guys what happened last night," Joni began breathlessly. "Beau came over! He actually apologized for going to the party without me."

"You're kidding!" cried Su-Su loudly. Then she clamped a hand over her mouth and peered around.

"Don't worry, nobody's around," Joni said impatiently. She was bursting with excitement. "But that's not all that happened, either. Promise you won't tell."

"Of course we won't tell," Su-Su insisted. She didn't act the least bit concerned that someone would see them now. "Come on, Joni. What happened?"

Joni took a deep breath and looked from one of her best friends to the other. "Okay. Here goes. He kissed me!"

"That's great," said Crystal. "But, uh, hasn't he kissed you before?"

"Of course he has," Joni said. "But this kiss was special. It was the most incredible kiss ever. And then do you know what I told him?"

Crystal and Su-Su shook their heads. "Come on. We're dying," begged Su-Su.

Joni was glad she had such fabulously good friends, because she knew if she didn't have someone to tell this to, she would absolutely explode. "You can't ever breathe a word of this. I told him I had a better nickname for him than Schwartzy. *The World's Best Kisser!*"

"Oh, Joni! That's so romantic!" cried Crystal, slumping dramatically against the steps as if she were fainting. "You see?" she said, popping up again. "I told you everything was going to work out all right, and it did." She smiled so widely that her dimple appeared in her left cheek.

"Right," said Su-Su. "And *I* told you that your imagination was going berserk."

"Okay, okay, so I was wrong," Joni said. "I probably don't need to leave a message on Boy Talk anymore, but I'm still going to do the hot line with you. We'd better hurry if we're going to get these flyers up before someone sees us."

The girls divided up the flyers and hurried off in different directions. Joni took the first floor of the building, and she looked over the flyer one more time as she headed down the hall, running a finger along the row of hearts at the top. They looked totally professional.

She thumbtacked one on the main bulletin board next to the office, and left a stack of them on the sink in the girls' bathroom. Then she began taping them above all the drinking fountains on that floor.

Just as she was reaching up to tape a flyer over the drinking fountain beside the office, Mrs. Carlyle, the school secretary, stepped out through the office door and started up the hall toward Joni.

Joni's heart almost stopped as she quickly ducked and took a drink of water. She couldn't take a chance on *anyone* seeing her post the flyers. No one could find out that she, Crystal, and Su-Su were behind Boy Talk. She watched out of the corner of her eye until Mrs. Carlyle turned a corner. Then with a sigh of relief she finished taping up the flyer.

"I left a bunch in the cafeteria," said Crystal when the girls met again on the front steps just before the bell.

"And I put one on every table in the Media Center," added Su-Su.

"I can't wait for kids to start calling," said Joni. "But I'm so nervous."

"Me, too," said Su-Su, twirling a strand of red hair around her finger.

"Me three," said Crystal. "But it's too late to turn back now. The word is out."

Joni thought the school day would last forever. *Everybody* was talking about Boy Talk. As Joni headed to her locker before class, she saw Marissa Pauley holding a flyer. Marissa waved it in the air when she saw Joni coming down the hall.

"Joni, check this out! We can call a hot-line number and get advice about guys," she said excitedly. "Look. It's called Boy Talk, and here's the number." She pointed to the phone number printed on the sheet.

Joni felt chills of excitement race up and down her back. It was working!

"Wow, let me see that," she said, trying her best to act surprised. She took the flyer and pretended to read it.

"We can call after school Monday through Friday," said Joni. "Great! Maybe I'll give it a try."

Marissa nodded. "Me, too! I've got to show this to Lisa and Traci."

Joni collapsed with relief against her locker as Marissa took the flyer back and hurried down the hall.

Everywhere Joni went, she saw kids standing in the halls reading the flyers and passing them around in class. She faked being as surprised and curious and thrilled as everybody else.

Finally the bell rang, dismissing classes for the day. Joni, Crystal, and Su-Su rushed to Crystal's house and quickly taped Mr. Britton's message on Joni's tape player. Then they recorded their own message on the answering machine.

At exactly three-thirty they gathered around the desk, snapped the tape to record Boy Talk calls into the answering machine, and waited nervously for the phone to ring.

Five minutes went by. The girls stared at the machine in silence.

"What if nobody calls?" Crystal asked finally.

"Give it a chance," said Su-Su. "Some kids may not even be home from school yet."

Joni watched the minute hand crawl slowly around the face of her watch. She didn't want to admit it to the others, but she was just as worried as Crystal. So what if everyone at school had acted excited about Boy Talk? That didn't mean they would actually call.

Ten minutes passed. Then fifteen. Still the phone

was silent. *Maybe no one will call after all*, Joni thought. *All our plans and hard work were for nothing.*

Suddenly the phone jangled, and the girls jumped to attention.

Joni gulped hard. "Oh, my gosh! It's ringing! Somebody's actually *calling!*"

After the third ring, there was a loud click. "Hello, welcome to Boy Talk. Thank you ever so much for ringing up."

Joni choked back a huge laugh that threatened to erupt at the sound of Su-Su's thick, super-fake-sounding English accent. She didn't dare look at either of her friends in case she broke up. Instead she tried to concentrate on Su-Su's voice as it went on explaining how to leave a message. Finally the beep sounded.

"Okay. Who's the joker behind this?" snapped a nasty, familiar voice. "I know this isn't for real, and I'm going to find out what's really going on. Just watch me!"

Joni heard the sound of giggling in the background just before the caller hung up. "That had to be April Mathis!" Joni cried. "I'd know her voice anywhere."

"Yeah," said Crystal. "April and her zillion snobby friends. Probably Molly Triola and Kristin Murphy and the rest of them."

"That's all we need," Su-Su said in disgust. "April

just can't stand having something going on that she's not part of."

"And if she ever finds out we're running Boy Talk, she'll make our lives miserable," Joni added.

Suddenly the phone rang again. The girls waited tensely while the voice with the bogus English accent gave instructions.

"Cross your fingers that it isn't April again," Joni whispered.

But this time there was the click of a receiver being hung up right after the beep.

"What do you think?" asked Su-Su, frowning. "Was it her?"

Joni shrugged. "Maybe. Or it could have been someone who was just curious and called to see who would answer."

"Maybe it was somebody who wanted to talk but lost her nerve," offered Crystal.

"Let's see if she calls back," said Joni. She stared hard at the phone, willing it to ring.

To her surprise, it did. There was a long silence after the beep.

Finally a girl's trembling voice said, "Hi, this is … this is Sneaking Around, and I have a *big problem*."

Joni held her breath as she, Crystal, and Su-Su moved closer to listen.

Chapter Six

Sneaking Around cleared her throat nervously. "There's this cute boy in my health class," she began, "and I've had a crush on him ever since school started. He's really nice, and he talks to me a lot. I kept hoping he'd ask me out, but he never did. I always wondered if he already had a girlfriend."

Sneaking Around paused, and Joni and her friends exchanged grins. Their first caller was on the line!

"Then we were at the same party last Saturday night," Sneaking Around continued.

Joni blinked in surprise. Was Sneaking Around talking about April's party? She hadn't heard about anyone else having a party that night.

"We talked for a long time, and he told me all

kinds of things, like wrestling is his favorite sport," Sneaking Around went on. "We got separated for a while, but just when I was getting ready to leave he found me again, and he actually asked me out! Not only that, but he asked me right in front of three of his friends. I couldn't believe it. Of course I said yes.

"The next morning I called two of my girlfriends and told them the big news. I could hardly wait to tell more people when I got to school today. But then in health class this morning, he asked me not to tell anybody about our date. He didn't say why. He just wanted me to keep quiet.

"I didn't know what to say. At first all I could think was that he didn't want anyone to see us together, that something was wrong with me. But the more I thought about it, the more I decided that he probably had a good reason, so I went along with it. But that was only the beginning. Now I'm getting to the bad part."

Sneaking Around paused again. "At lunch I saw the girls I had told Sunday morning, and they said they'd already spread the news around to some of my other friends. What if it gets back to him that so many kids know? *What should I do?*"

Joni stared at the answering machine as the caller hung up. A funny feeling was gathering in the pit of her stomach.

"Did you hear that?" she said just above a whisper. "Sneaking Around went to April's party. The one *we* weren't invited to. The one Beau Maguire *did* go to!"

"So?" asked Crystal.

"You aren't thinking that Sneaking Around was talking about Beau, are you?" asked Su-Su, making a face. "Not after the way he kissed you last night."

Joni took a deep breath. "I don't know what I'm thinking. But I'm really confused."

"Why?" asked Su-Su.

"Promise you won't tell?" Joni asked.

"For heaven's sake, Joni, you always say that. We're your best friends, remember?" said Su-Su. "We never tell anything you ask us not to."

"Right," said Crystal. "You know you can trust us."

Joni nodded slowly. "I know. I've said this before, but one minute I think everything's cool between Beau and me, and then something happens that makes me wonder if he wants to break up."

"I still don't get it," said Su-Su. "What does Sneaking Around have to do with you and Beau? Lots of kids went to April's party."

"Yeah, but she said this cute boy had three friends, remember? You know as well as I do that Beau is always with Twister, Parker, and Jason. He does everything with them when he's not with me."

"Lots of people have three friends," said Crystal.

"But she also said wrestling is his favorite sport,"

said Joni. "Beau is captain of the wrestling team!"

"But she didn't say he was on the wrestling team," Su-Su pointed out. "She said wrestling was his favorite sport. That's different. Maybe he meant on TV. I think you're getting paranoid."

"Exactly." said Crystal. "Have you actually *seen* Beau flirting with anyone?"

"No," Joni admitted.

"See?" Su-Su snapped. "Didn't he come over last night and apologize for going to April's party? And didn't he kiss you? How can you explain that?"

"I can't," said Joni. "Unless maybe he came over to break up and lost his nerve."

Crystal rolled her eyes. "So he kissed you instead? Sure, that makes a lot of sense."

"Well, maybe he had a guilty conscience about asking Sneaking Around out. Or maybe he likes both of us." Joni threw up her hands. "I don't know how to explain it. It's just a feeling I have."

"I do, too," said Su-Su. "My feeling is that you're crazy!"

"All I know is, Beau could be the boy Sneaking Around is talking about, and he could be going to take her out behind my back!" Joni said angrily. "In fact, I'm going to use your other phone, Crystal, and leave my own message on Boy Talk. I'm going to tell Sneaking Around off big time and order her to leave Beau *alone*!"

"You can't do that!" shrieked Su-Su, throwing herself across the answering machine. "You don't know who Sneaking Around is! You don't even know if Beau is the boy she's talking about. There are almost eight hundred kids in our school. It could be *anybody*."

For a moment Joni didn't say anything. A picture of Beau strolling into the movie theater with another girl flashed into her mind. Joni couldn't see her face, but she could see Beau put his arm around her just as the movie started. Tears filled her eyes.

How dare Beau Maguire sneak around and take out someone behind my back? she thought.

Crystal put a sympathetic hand on Joni's arm. "Look at it this way, Joni. Today is only the first day of Boy Talk. If you call in and put a message on the machine and April recognizes your voice, she might figure out that we're the ones behind it. That would blow everything, and you might never find out who Sneaking Around is. *And* April would make us all the laughingstock of Sunshine Beach Middle School."

"Yeah, Joni. Chill out, okay?" Su-Su urged.

Joni took a deep breath and let it out slowly. "Okay," she said. "I'll wait. But just until I find out who Sneaking Around is."

Chapter Seven

For the rest of the hour Boy Talk got almost more calls than the answering machine could handle. Some kids called just to listen, but more and more calls were from girls recording messages. Some of them were asking for advice. Others were giving it.

Beep.

"Hi, this is Dying to Be Kissed. I think this boy I like is getting ready to ask me out. What will I do if he wants to kiss me? I don't know how to kiss a boy. I've only kissed my relatives! Help! I need someone to tell me how to kiss romantically. *Pleeeze!*"

Beep.

"For the first time in my life, a boy finally likes me. He even asked me out! I sort of like him. The trouble is, he's a nerd. If I go out with him, everybody will think I'm a nerd, too. Should I go, or shouldn't I? Call me Not a Nerd."

The next two calls were from kids who only listened, but the third call was another message.

Beep.

"This is a message for Dying to Be Kissed from Been There. I know just how you feel. Before I got my first real kiss I tried practicing. First I kissed my mirror. My eyes crossed! Next I kissed my pillow and almost smothered. I was scared to death that when the big moment came I'd do it wrong. Guess what? I didn't. It was easy."

"I just love this!" cried Su-Su as soon as Been There hung up. "It's working! Kids are actually calling in."

"I wish I could disguise my voice the way you can, Su-Su," said Crystal. "I'm dying to record some advice."

"Me, too," Joni muttered. "I've got plenty of advice for Sneaking Around."

"I'm serious," Crystal insisted. "Not a Nerd ought to decide what *she* thinks about this guy, and not worry about what everybody else thinks. I'd really like to tell her that."

"I know you would," said Su-Su. "You're a regular 'Dear Abby.'" She was thoughtful for a moment. "If you really want to help out Not a Nerd, tell me what you want to say. I'll call from the phone in your room and disguise my voice."

"You'd really do that?" Crystal asked gleefully.

Su-Su nodded.

Crystal grabbed a notepad off her father's desk and began scribbling. When she was finished, she tore the page off the pad and handed it to Su-Su. "Thanks a million," she said, beaming.

Su-Su disappeared. A few minutes later, the phone beside the answering machine rang and the greeting message came on.

Beep.

"Hi, y'all. This here is Southern Belle callin' for Not a Nerd."

Joni slapped a hand over her mouth to keep from roaring with laughter at Su-Su's thick southern accent.

"You shouldn't worry about what other kids think about this boy if you like him. Ya heah? You might miss findin' the man of your dreams."

"That's not exactly what I wrote down," said Crystal when Su-Su came back into the room. "But I loved it!"

"Your accent was great," said Joni.

Su-Su grinned. "I think next time I'll do Whoopi Goldberg," she said.

The phone rang again.

Beep.

"This is a message for Sneaking Around from Get the Scoop."

Joni leaned closer to the answering machine to listen.

"If you want my advice, you should tell this guy that you already told some of your friends about your date before he asked you to keep it a secret. Unless he's a real jerk, he'll understand. Then ask him *why* he wants to sneak around. That's what I'd do."

"Pretty good advice, if you ask me," said Crystal, shrugging.

Joni nodded. It made a lot of sense. Sneaking Around should talk to the guy immediately. But if he really was Beau, then Joni needed to know why he was sneaking around, too. And the sooner the better!

"If she does it, I hope she calls back and tells us what he said," said Joni.

Beep.

"I've got advice for Sneaking Around. This is Suspicious. I'd be careful about going out with someone who wants to sneak around. What kind of guy would do a thing like that, anyway? I think you ought to break the date."

"More good advice," said Su-Su when Suspicious hung up.

Joni frowned at the answering machine. Both Get the Scoop and Suspicious had offered great suggestions. But both tactics could backfire for her, Joni. What if Sneaking Around asked her boyfriend-to-be why he wanted to date on the sly, and he said it was because he hadn't gotten up the nerve to break up with his girlfriend yet? And what if Sneaking Around convinced him to go ahead and do it?

On the other hand, if Sneaking Around followed Suspicious's advice and broke her date, he might think Sneaking Around was playing hard to get. That could make him want to go out with her more than ever.

Either way, I could lose, Joni thought miserably. The only question left was, whose advice would Sneaking Around decide to take?

Chapter Eight

As soon as Boy Talk was over for the day, Joni went straight home. She ran upstairs to her room and ran her finger along the row of Lindsey Jones mysteries in her bookcase, looking for *The Poison Pen Letters*. In that book, Lindsey had been hired to find the person who was sending hate mail to a beautiful actress. She had to identify him before the mysterious writer sent a deadly letter bomb, the way he or she had to another actress.

It had been a long time since Joni had read *The Poison Pen Letters*. She needed to refresh her memory on exactly how Lindsey figured out who the mysterious letter writer was. Maybe she could use the same technique to identify Sneaking Around.

She was sprawled across her bed reading when the

phone rang. She picked up the receiver on her bed-side table and started to say hello, but her mother was already on the line. It sounded like Mr. Grasso from the *Sunshine Beach Citizen* on the other end. Her mother worked part-time as a photographer for the paper.

Joni hung up softly and went back to her reading.

A minute later there was a soft tap on the door. "Joni, may I come in?"

"Sure, Mom."

Joni glanced up as her mother entered the room. Mrs. Sparkman was tall and thin and wore her dark hair in a French braid. She was dressed in jeans and already had her camera bag slung over her shoulder. Then Joni saw Hannah behind her. Hannah, who was a carbon copy of their mother, complete with the dark French braid down her back, had a big grin on her face. Joni got a sinking feeling in the pit of her stomach.

"Honey, that was Mr. Grasso," Mrs. Sparkman said. "I have to go out on an assignment. There's been an accident across town, and he wants me to shoot it." Then looking apologetic, she added, "You don't mind keeping an eye on Hannah, do you? I won't be gone long."

Joni shot a warning look at her little sister. "Only if she stays out of my room," she replied.

"Mo-om, make her let me in her room. Pleeeease,"

begged Hannah. "I'll be scared in the family room all by myself."

Joni thought it was amazing how Hannah could force tears into her eyes and make her chin quiver whenever she wanted something from one of their parents. And she was doing that now. Naturally, their mom did exactly what Hannah wanted her to do. She ordered Joni to let Hannah stay in her room until someone else got home.

"Stay out of my things," Joni said sharply as soon as her mother had left.

"I brought stuff to color," said Hannah. She sat down at the desk and began drawing with a Magic Marker.

Good, Joni thought, sticking her nose back into her book. She was getting to the good part and didn't want any more interruptions.

"What's this?" asked a small voice a few minutes later.

Joni was horrified to see Hannah was standing beside the bed holding up a Boy Talk flyer. "Where did you get that?" Joni demanded, grabbing the flyer away from her little sister. "I told you not to touch any of my things! You were snooping again, weren't you?"

Hannah ignored the question. "Did you have to call Boy Talk? How come? Doesn't Beau love you anymore?"

"None of your business," snapped Joni. "Now sit in that chair and be quiet. I'm trying to read."

"I'll tell Mom you were mean to me," said Hannah. She smiled sweetly at Joni.

"You'd better not," warned Joni. "Not if you know what's good for you."

"And I'll tell her I saw you and Beau kissing on the patio last night, and I'll—"

"Okay, okay," Joni said, slapping the book shut. She didn't need any of the hassles that Hannah's big mouth could cause. "How about a game of Pictionary in the family room until Mom gets back?"

"That would be fun!" Hannah said, a note of triumph in her voice.

It was after dinner before Joni got back to her room and her Lindsey Jones mystery. At two o'clock in the morning, she turned off her flashlight and tossed the book on the nightstand. She was exhausted, but now she had a plan for finding out who Sneaking Around was.

The next morning before school, Joni hurried to her locker. Marissa Pauley's locker was next to hers, and she was waiting there when Marissa arrived. Even though they weren't close friends, they were pretty friendly, and Marissa just might have the information she needed.

"Hi, Marissa," Joni said, giving her a big smile. "How's it going?"

Marissa shrugged and began working her combination. "Okay, I guess. School is so boring this year."

Perfect! thought Joni. She quickly flipped the switch on her tape recorder, which she had hidden in her belt bag.

"Speaking of boring," Joni went on, "I hear April's party Saturday night was a big flop."

Marissa looked at her in surprise. "I didn't think so. It was the best party since school started. Who told you it was a flop?"

Joni pretended to think. "I can't remember now," she said finally. "I heard lots of kids saying it, though. I guess not very many people showed up. At least that's what I heard."

"I don't know who told you that, either," said Marissa, frowning. "The place was packed."

"Oh, yeah? So who was there?" Joni asked. She was about to get the information she needed, and she couldn't believe how cool she sounded.

"Well, April, of course, and her crowd. You know, Molly Triola and Kristin Murphy, and all the cheerleading squad. Toni Biagi was there, and Alison Hamel and Hope Seymour and Megan Scully and Ashley Malott, and…"

Joni listened as Marissa recited a long list of girls. She only knew about half of them, but that was okay. Once she had their names on her tape recorder, she could get to work. One of them had to be Sneaking Around.

"There were lots of guys there, too," Marissa went on. "Jordan Losen and Steven Diaz and Micah LaMontagne and Evan Byrnes and Dan Turpin and Parker Hatch and Jason Duffy and Beau—" She stopped and gave Joni a horrified look. "You . . . you did know that Beau went, didn't you?"

Joni shrugged. "Sure," she said offhandedly. She thought about asking Marissa who Beau had been talking to at the party, but she changed her mind. She might start freaking out. And there was a chance Marissa would spread it around that she was checking up on Beau. If that got back to Beau, he might decide to break up with her for sure.

No, she thought. *I have to stay cool if I'm going to crack this case.*

"Well, I've got to go now," Joni said, closing her locker. "See you around, Marissa."

Instead of heading in the direction of her own first-period class, Joni made a detour down another hall. That was where the health room was. Sneaking Around had said she talked to the boy during health class, and Beau had health first period.

The hall was packed with kids pushing and shoving the way they always did. Joni let the crowd carry her along. As she got closer to the health room, she looked around for a spot where she could stop and watch who went inside without being noticed—especially by Beau. She would die if he caught her spying.

Her plan was to write down the names of all the girls she knew as they went into the health room and compare them with the names from the party. Then she would make a list of the names that matched and try to identify the ones she didn't know.

Her gaze fell on a drinking fountain across the hall. There was a long line of kids waiting to get a drink. Perfect. It would be natural for her to get in line at a drinking fountain. No one would suspect that she was actually there to spy. And if she saw Beau coming up the hall, she could duck away and pretend she was searching for something in her backpack.

Students were beginning to enter the health classroom. Joni held her notebook closer to her chest so that no one would notice that she was taking notes and looked nervously up and down the hall.

At first she didn't know any of the girls who entered the room. Then Cami Petre went in, but Cami hadn't gone to the party. At least, not according to Marissa. Lisa Berkowitz and Christie Sharp weren't among the names Marissa had rattled off, either. But Hope Seymour was. And Jill McDonald. And Jessica Lloyd.

Joni darted a glance at the clock at the end of the hall.

There were only two minutes left until the bell. She was going to be late.

Joni quickly retraced her steps down the hall, glancing down at the names she had scribbled in her notebook. Her heart sank. Only three. Hope Seymour. Jill McDonald. Jessica Lloyd. Was one of them Sneaking Around?

Joni didn't have time to work on her list of suspicious names for the rest of the school day. She decided to do it as soon as she got home from Crystal's house. With any luck, she would figure out Sneaking Around's identity and put part two of her plan into action.

At three-thirty that afternoon, Joni, Crystal, and Su-Su had barely popped the Boy Talk tape into the answering machine and sat down around the desk when the first call came in.

Beep.

"Hi, everybody. This is Sneaking Around again. Guess what? I have a new problem."

Chapter Nine

"I took Get the Scoop's advice, and now I wish I hadn't," said Sneaking Around. She sounded as if she were about to cry.

Joni caught her breath and exchanged nervous glances with Crystal and Su-Su.

"I did just what she said," Sneaking Around went on. "When I saw him in health class this morning I told him that I hadn't known he wanted our date to be a secret when I told a couple of my friends. And they didn't know it was supposed to be a secret when they told a few more girls."

She paused, and Joni's pulse raced.

"Come on, what did he say?" Joni murmured impatiently. She clenched her fists as she waited for

Sneaking Around to continue recording her message.

"At first he acted a little mad," she said. "Then I said I didn't understand why he didn't want anybody to know he was taking me out. I asked him if he was ashamed to be seen with me."

"Wow," said Crystal. "Sneaking Around has more guts than I thought."

"Shhhh! I want to hear this," said Joni.

"He said that wasn't it and he liked me a lot. But listen to this." Her voice quivered. "He has another girlfriend, but he's been thinking about breaking up with her. He told me he thought our date might help him make up his mind who he likes best."

Joni gripped the desk to steady herself. Her worst nightmare was coming true!

"Part of me feels awful that he's using me as a test to decide if he likes another girl," Sneaking Around went on. "Another part of me wants him to like me best and break up with his girlfriend. My problem is, I don't know if I should take a chance and go out with him, or if I should tell him to forget the whole thing. I'm afraid I'm just going to get hurt."

"Poor Sneaking Around," said Crystal. "I feel sorry for her."

"What do you mean, poor Sneaking Around?" demanded Joni. She jumped to her feet and glared at

Crystal. "What about *me*? I'm the one he's going to dump!"

"Come on, Joni," said Su-Su. "You still don't know for sure that Sneaking Around is talking about Beau."

"Well, I'm going to find out once and for all," said Joni. "You guys can keep listening to Boy Talk, but I'm going home. I'm going to call Beau and find out what's going on."

Crystal and Su-Su watched silently as she picked up her books.

"Are you sure you want to do that?" Su-Su asked.

Joni nodded. "My mind's made up. I need to find out, and it's now or never."

"Gosh, Joni. I hope everything's okay," said Crystal.

"Me, too," said Su-Su. "Call us as soon as you talk to him. Okay?"

Joni nodded and left for home. She stopped on the sidewalk in front of Crystal's house and thought about going to Beau's house instead of calling him on the phone. She would be able to tell by looking at his eyes if he was lying to her. But what if he *did* lie or said he wanted to break up with her, and she started to cry? *No*, she thought. *I can't let him see me cry.*

It would be better to call. She knew that Beau had

the house to himself after school. Both his parents worked, and his older brother had always had football practice. Luckily there was no one home at her house, either. There was a note on the fridge from her mother, saying she had taken Hannah to a dentist appointment.

Joni grabbed an apple out of the basket on the kitchen table and headed for her room, trying to decide what she was going to say to Beau.

I could just come right out and ask him if he's going out with someone else Saturday night, she thought.

The idea made her cringe. What if he admitted it? Then what would she say? "Have a great time"?

Besides, she knew how much Beau hated it when she acted jealous or possessive. He might get mad and tell her to get lost. She couldn't stand it if he did that. She cared about him too much.

Memories of all their special times together ran through her mind. Quiet times when they had sat on her front steps in the moonlight and talked about important things. Like how they both wanted to make a difference in the world when they grew up and how much they worried about what was happening to the environment.

They had shared lots of fun times, too. Fireworks on the beach. Dressing up like reindeer and riding on the Sunshine Beach Middle School float in the holiday parade. Seeing movies together and hanging out with their friends. Her heart ached at the thought of all that ending forever.

Joni sat down on the edge of her bed and stared at the phone on her nightstand as another horrible thought came into mind. What would everyone at school think if Beau broke up with her for another girl? It would be so humiliating. Maybe she should wait a little longer and see what happened.

"But I *have* to find out," she told herself.

She reached for the phone and hesitated. "What would Lindsey Jones do?" she wondered out loud. She knew the answer to that. Lindsey would play it cool. She would start out being nice and sweet and try to trick Beau into giving himself away.

Joni picked up the receiver and punched in Beau's number before she could lose her nerve.

The line was busy.

She forced herself to wait five minutes before she tried again. It was still busy.

Joni bit hard into her apple and paced the floor.

Who could he be talking to for such a long time? she wondered. Beau didn't usually like talking on the phone that much.

Was he talking to Sneaking Around?

She decided to wait ten minutes before she tried again. The hands on her watch moved with excruciating slowness.

Blap-blap-blap.

The busy signal hurt Joni's pride as well as her ears.

He must be talking to a girl! she thought miserably and slammed down the phone.

She wished she had stayed at Boy Talk until four-thirty and then brought her friends home with her before she called. She needed them for moral support. They always made her feel better. Crystal was full of sympathy and good advice, and Su-Su would clown around until she got at least a smile. But her friends weren't here now. She would have to do this all by herself.

Joni tried four more times and got four more busy signals. With each one, she got more worried. And more angry, too. How could Beau *do* a thing like this to her after all they had meant to each other? Finally she heard the phone ringing.

"Maguire residence. This is Beau."

She bit her lip and tried to stay calm, even though her heart was beating like crazy.

"Hi, Beau. I've been trying to call you for ages, but your line was busy." The instant the words were out, she regretted them. Beau would probably think she was monitoring his phone calls and be mad. She wished she had thought of a better way to start the conversation.

"Oh, hi, Joni," Beau replied, sounding sheepish.

"Um, well, I was talking to my mom. She called from her office to ask me to do some stuff for her."

Joni's mouth dropped open. She couldn't believe what she was hearing. What did he think she was, stupid?

"You were talking to your mother for almost an *hour?*" she exploded into the phone. "Come on, Beau!"

She knew this time she'd totally blown her cool, but it didn't matter. Beau was definitely lying.

"No, honest," he said. "It was my mom. She, uh…she had to put me on hold for a few minutes. Hey, I'm really glad you called, though. Want to do something Friday night?"

Caught off guard, Joni hesitated. She wanted desperately to believe that he wasn't lying about talking to his mom. The excuse sounded so bogus. Still, there was a chance he might be telling the truth. And maybe Crystal and Su-Su were right when they'd accused her of overreacting to Sneaking Around when she didn't even know for sure if Beau was the boy Sneaking Around was talking about. Lindsey Jones would probably say that all her evidence against Beau was circumstantial.

"I thought I might rent a movie and come over," Beau added. "Then we could order in a pizza."

Joni thought that over in silence. *Rent a movie? Come over?* Why did he want to do that? They always went *out* to a movie on Friday night. So did everyone else in Sunshine Beach Middle School. It was the big night of the week to see and be seen.

It isn't just Sneaking Around he doesn't want to be seen with in public, she thought, shaking her head in disbelief. *Now he doesn't want to be seen with me, either!*

She bit her lower lip to keep it steady. "I can't do anything this Friday night. I have to baby-sit," she said, praying her lie would trap him into giving himself away. "How about Saturday instead?"

There was a long silence on the other end of the line. Joni held her breath and gripped the receiver with both hands. Would he tell her he had a date with another girl?

"I can't on Saturday. We're having a bunch of company. Um ... relatives. It's my aunt and uncle and my two cousins," he added, the words tumbling out. "They're coming in from out of town. My folks would go ballistic if I told them I wouldn't be home Saturday. So I guess ... I guess I'll see you later, okay? Bye."

Lame! Joni thought, slamming down the receiver. *Definitely lame! He's lying because he's going out with Sneaking Around!*

She collapsed across her bed and started sobbing into her pillow.

Chapter Ten

The shrill ring of the telephone startled Joni a few minutes later. She sat up and wiped the tears off her face with the back of her hand.

Should she answer? She hesitated, then reached for the phone.

"Joni, it's Su-Su. Did you talk to Beau yet? Crystal and I have been going crazy waiting to hear from you."

"Oh, hi, Su-Su." Joni cradled the phone against her shoulder. "I just talked to him a few minutes ago. Would you believe his line was busy for nearly an hour?"

"So what happened? What did he say? Is he going out with Sneaking Around?" cried Su-Su.

"He didn't admit it, but I know he is," Joni said

sadly. "And get this. Instead of going to the movies Friday night, the way we always do, he wanted to *rent* a movie and come over here. Then I made up a story that I had to baby-sit Friday night and asked if he wanted to do something Saturday night instead. He gave me a totally lame excuse. He said he had relatives visiting from out of town."

"You mean you didn't come right out and ask him what was going on the way you said you would?" asked Crystal.

Joni sighed. "No, I decided to try to trick him into giving himself away. And in a way, I guess he did."

"It sounds pretty bogus to me," said Su-Su. "He really is thinking of breaking up with you, isn't he? Why else would he try to make dates with both of you on the same weekend and not want to be seen in public with either of you?"

"Exactly," said Joni miserably.

"What are you going to do now?" asked Su-Su.

"I wish I knew," Joni admitted. "Did anyone call Boy Talk with ideas for Sneaking Around's latest problem?"

"Boy, did they ever," said Su-Su. "At least six girls called to say things like: 'Go for it.' 'This could be your big chance.'"

"Didn't anybody care about the girl he's going to cheat on?" Joni asked indignantly.

"Uh, not really," said Su-Su. "One girl called in to

tell Sneaking Around she should be careful. If he was the kind of guy who would sneak around behind his girlfriend's back, he might do the same thing to her. That was it."

"So I guess that means Sneaking Around's probably not going to break their date," said Joni, her spirits plummeting. Tears blurred her eyes again. "*She's* going out with him this weekend, and *I'm* not!"

"Maybe you should leave a message for Sneaking Around on Boy Talk after all," suggested Crystal.

"Boy Talk is over for today, and by tomorrow it may be too late to change her mind," said Joni. Her voice began to shake, but she quickly got it under control again. She wasn't going to give Beau up without a fight.

As soon as she hung up with her friends, Joni turned on her tape recorder and wrote down the names of all twenty-four of the girls Marissa had said were at April's party. She knew sixteen of them. That meant there were eight girls at the party she didn't know.

Next she checked the list she had made outside the health room door. Only three of the girls she had recognized were on the party list.

Joni threw down her pen and sighed with exasperation. This was going to be a bigger job than she had thought.

Before school the next morning, she called Crystal

and Su-Su aside by the bike rack and showed them the party lists.

Crystal's face clouded immediately. "Evan Byrnes and Alison Hamel. I knew they'd be there together," she grumbled.

Joni gave Crystal a sympathetic look. "I put a check mark beside the names of all the girls I don't know," she said. "Do you guys know any of them?"

"Well, I know Megan Scully and Jessica Nealy," said Su-Su. "They're in my math class. And I know Missy Glenn and Brittany Preston from history."

"And I know Ashley Malott and Shannon Terry," said Crystal. "We have English class together."

Joni sighed with relief. "Okay! Now we're getting somewhere. Be on the lookout for them and point them out to me."

"Sure," said Su-Su. Then she glanced over Joni's shoulder and frowned. "Don't look now, but I think we're getting company."

Joni couldn't help looking. April Mathis was heading straight toward them. Molly Triola and Kristin Murphy were with her, and so was Brenna Flatt. As usual, April's three best friends had tried to dress as much like April as they could. Today April had on a violet ribbed knit tank top under a blue-and-violet mini madras dress. Practically the only difference between April's outfits and the ones that Molly, Kristin, and Brenna wore was the color.

"Hi, guys," April said brightly when they came up. She held out a Boy Talk flyer. "Do any of you know anything about this?"

Joni did a double take, feeling flames of guilt shoot up her face.

"Of course not," Su-Su said.

April cocked an eyebrow at Su-Su. "What did you say?" she asked sweetly.

Suddenly Joni knew what April was doing. She was listening for a voice that sounded like the one on the Boy Talk message. Had she recognized Su-Su?

"She said we don't," Joni interjected before Su-Su could open her mouth again and give herself away. "What makes you think we'd know anything about it?"

April's eyes flicked to Joni. "I'm just checking it out," she said with a shrug. Then she looked straight at Su-Su again as she went on talking. "I think whoever is doing this goes to Sunshine Beach Middle School. I'm going to find out who these losers are if it's the last thing I ever do."

Joni, Crystal, and Su-Su watched in silence as April and her clones moved on to another group of girls.

"She knows!" said Crystal as soon as they were out of earshot. "Did you see the way she looked at Su-Su? I *know* she knows!"

"No, she doesn't," said Joni. "Otherwise she

wouldn't be talking to so many other people. Look, she's stopping Marissa Pauley now."

They watched as April and her friends moved around the school grounds, stopping at each group of girls they came to and holding up the Boy Talk flyer.

"You have to admit, it's sort of funny," said Joni. "April can't stand not being in on every single thing going on at school."

When the first bell rang, the girls headed in separate directions for their lockers.

Joni said hi to Marissa and got out the books for her morning classes. Then she started walking toward the Spanish room, her mind still on April.

"He is *so* cute! I still can't believe that he asked me out."

Joni's eyes widened. *I know that voice*, she told herself. *That's Sneaking Around!*

Glancing over her shoulder, Joni spotted two girls walking in the opposite direction. They had passed right by her. And it had to have been one of them she had heard.

Whirling around, she joined the line of kids going their way. She would probably be late for Spanish, but she didn't care. Now was her big chance to find out Sneaking Around's identity!

"Oops! Excuse me," she said, cutting in front of a group of slow-moving kids.

She caught up with the two girls, and hurried along behind them. She couldn't see their faces, but one girl had shoulder-length blond hair and the other girl's red-brown hair was done in a French braid.

Walking as close as she dared, she strained to catch more of their conversation.

"So you've definitely made up your mind? You're going to go out with him?" asked the brown-haired girl.

The blond girl nodded. "I can't wait for you to meet him. When he's ready, I mean," she added quickly.

"Is he cute?" asked the other girl.

"You can see for yourself," the blonde replied. "When I go into health, check out the boy sitting in the second seat of the third row. That's him!"

Joni's heart sank. This had to be Sneaking Around. She was headed for health class, and the guy she was talking about wasn't ready to meet her friends.

Just then the girl glanced over her shoulder to say hi to someone, and Joni saw her face. She was pretty, but not gorgeous. Her hair was nice, but not great. *She's just sort of . . . normal,* Joni thought, feeling a little disappointed. *My competition is no big deal.* Her clothes were nothing to get excited about, either. Jeans. A multicolored vest over a plain white T-shirt.

He must see something special in her, Joni thought. *But what?*

She slowed down to let the two girls get farther in front of her. Her worst fears were coming true. Still, there was a tiny chance that the boy Sneaking Around was talking about wasn't Beau. Filled with dread, Joni marched down the hall. She was this close. She had to find out.

The blond girl waved good-bye to her friend at the health room door and went inside.

Joni could feel her pulse pounding in her temples. She took a deep breath and kept on going. Passing the open door, she looked in. It was almost time for the bell, and the class was filling up. She quickly counted across to the third row and down to the second seat. Her heart sank. It was Beau Maguire, all right. He was smiling at the blond girl as she entered the room.

Now Joni knew for sure that Beau was cheating on her.

And she had finally found Sneaking Around.

Chapter Eleven

Joni kept an eye out for Sneaking Around all morning. Each time classes changed, she scanned the halls in both directions for the girl with shoulder-length blond hair, jeans, and a bright-colored vest, but she didn't see her anywhere.

She met Crystal and Su-Su outside the cafeteria at noon. When she spotted them waiting for her, neither one was looking in her direction. Su-Su's eyes were closed, and she was swishing the hem of her long prairie dress in time to the music coming through her headphones. Crystal was running a brush through her honey-blond hair while she read the day's menu posted on the bulletin board outside the lunchroom door.

"Hey, guys! Guess what? I saw Sneaking Around!"

Joni cried, waving and rushing toward her friends. "And now I know for sure it's Beau she's been talking about."

Su-Su took off her headphones. "What?" she said.

"Come on. Let's get on the lunch line, and I'll tell you everything," said Joni.

They took trays and joined the long line of kids heading toward the steam tables. As they loaded their trays with burgers and fries, Joni explained about hearing Sneaking Around's voice in the hall and following her. Then, as the three of them found an empty table and sat down with their lunches, she told her friends the rest of the story.

"It was Beau, all right," Joni said, dropping her voice. "I kept my fingers crossed right up to the second I looked in the door that it would be somebody else, but it wasn't."

"That jerk," snapped Su-Su. "Does he really think he can get away with this?"

"What are you going to do now that you know he's definitely cheating on you?" asked Crystal. She put down her sandwich and looking at Joni sadly. The big dimple that appeared like magic when she smiled was nowhere in sight. "Are you going to break up with him?"

It was the question Joni had dreaded most. She sighed and looked helplessly at her friends.

"Probably," she said, trying to sound more determined than she felt. "I mean, it hurts so much to know that he's cheating on me. And it makes me furious too. But at the same time I'm really confused. I can't understand why he'd do a thing like this. It just doesn't seem like him."

"Maybe he gets his kicks out of sneaking around," said Su-Su, running her fingers through her long red hair. "You know, like it's a big thrill to get away with something."

Joni thought for a moment. "No, I don't think that's it," she said slowly. "He's really not that kind of person."

"Maybe his friends have something to do with it," said Crystal. "You know what creeps they are."

"That's a definite possibility," said Joni. Then something over Su-Su's shoulder caught her attention.

It was Sneaking Around and her brown-haired friend. They were carrying their lunch trays and looking for a table.

"Hey, guys, there she is!" hissed Joni. "Sneaking Around! Over there. The girl with the blond hair."

Crystal and Su-Su both looked where Joni was pointing.

"I know her," said Su-Su. "Her name's Megan Scully. She's in my math class."

"Megan Scully? That sounds familiar," said Joni. She whipped April's party list out of her belt bag and quickly scanned the names. "Here she is," she said, stopping halfway down the page.

Her heart was thudding. Now Sneaking Around not only had a face, she had a real name.

"I wouldn't have picked Megan Scully as being Beau's type in a million years," Su-Su said, shaking her head. "She's so quiet you hardly know she's in the class."

Crystal let out a whoop. "Compared to you, everybody's quiet," she said. Then she grinned at Su-Su to show she was teasing.

"So what else do you know about her?" asked Joni.

"Not much," said Su-Su. "She seems nice enough, but pretty boring. You're a much more interesting person."

"Thanks for the compliment, but that doesn't help the situation," Joni said dejectedly. She glanced back at Megan. "I just don't understand it. Megan Scully and I are total opposites. What made Beau want to date someone so different from me?"

"Why don't you just ask him?" asked Crystal. "He's over there near the window, horsing around with his buddies." Crystal nodded toward a table on the other side of the cafeteria.

Joni turned around. Beau was laughing loudly and talking to Twister, Parker, and Jason. She narrowed her eyes as she watched them, suddenly realizing what they were doing. They were having a belching contest!

"They're acting *so* immature," she muttered in disgust.

Just then, something seemed to catch Beau's eye. Joni couldn't see who or what it was at first because too many kids were in the way. Then Megan Scully came into view. She and her friend were still looking for a table. They were going to pass right by Beau's table! When they did, Beau gave Megan a huge grin and said something that Joni couldn't hear. Megan's face lit up, and she stopped for a moment, saying something back to Beau before moving on.

Joni just stared as Megan and her friend finally found a table and sat down Then she slapped her hand on her tray and jumped to her feet. "That does it!" she cried. "Did you see that? Beau was *flirting* with Megan Scully!"

Clenching her fists, she headed straight for Beau's table.

"Hey, Schwartzy, look who's coming," she heard Twister say.

But Beau had already seen her. He was looking at her in alarm as she marched toward him.

"Beau Maguire, I just saw you flirting with Megan Scully," she said angrily. "And I also know why you're busy Saturday night, and it isn't because you have relatives visiting. You're going out with her, aren't you?"

Out of the corner of her eye she saw Twister,

Parker, and Jason's mouths drop open at her outburst. She didn't care what they thought. She didn't care what the whole world thought!

"Where'd you hear a thing like that?" asked Beau. He shrugged and looked helplessly from one of his friends to the other as if it were the weirdest thing he'd ever heard.

"It's true, isn't it? You might as well admit it," Joni insisted.

Beau shifted uneasily in his seat. "I don't have to admit anything. I can't help it if you listen to stupid gossip."

"Hey, Schwartzy, tell your girlfriend to get off your back," said Jason. "She doesn't *own* you."

Beau looked uncomfortable.

"You don't have to tell me anything," Joni said angrily. "I don't want to talk to you ever again!"

She didn't wait for Beau's reaction. Whirling around, she stormed out of the cafeteria and headed for the girls' bathroom. Behind her, she heard two sets of footsteps racing down the hall.

"Joni! Wait!" cried Crystal.

"What happened?" asked Su-Su.

Joni turned slowly to face her friends. Tears were streaming down her face.

"I did it," she said almost in a whisper. "I just broke up with Beau."

Chapter Twelve

Crystal and Su-Su begged and pleaded, but Joni was too upset over breaking up with Beau to go to Crystal's house after school for Boy Talk. Even though they were her best friends, she just didn't feel like talking to anyone right now. Or listening to anyone else's problems, either. She had enough of her own.

When the phone rang that evening while she was trying to concentrate on her homework, she thought for an instant that it might be Beau, calling to apologize. He had apologized once before. Maybe he would do it again.

"Hello?" she said hopefully. Her heart sank when she heard Crystal's voice.

"Do you want the bad news or the horrible news

first?" Crystal asked. Then she added, "Actually, I'm not sure which one is the worst."

"Take your pick," Joni mumbled. "I can hardly wait. My day couldn't get much worse."

"Okay, here goes. April called Boy Talk this afternoon."

Joni rolled her eyes toward the ceiling. She couldn't care less about April. Not right now, anyway.

"She said, 'Don't think you can get away with this much longer. I know who you are, and I'm going to tell *everybody*,'" Crystal went on in a dramatic tone.

"You're kidding," said Joni, feeling a tiny spark of interest. "Do you think she really knows?"

"I'm not sure," Crystal admitted. "I mean, she might just be trying to scare us into stopping Boy Talk, since it's getting so much attention around school."

"What about Su-Su? Has April been trying to get her to talk again?" asked Joni.

"Not really," said Crystal. "Su-Su does have a class with her, though. But that's just the bad news. Are you ready for the horrible news?"

"As ready as I'll ever be." Joni sighed.

"The phone bill came today."

Alarms went off in Joni's head. She had been so worried about Beau and Sneaking Around that she had temporarily forgotten about the twenty-four dollars and five cents she owed Mr. Britton for her share of the call to Romance Rap.

"He went ballistic," said Crystal. "I mean *really* ballistic."

Joni's heart beat faster. "Gosh, Crystal, what did he do?"

"He yelled about how 900 numbers are a rip-off and I should have known better. I told him all three of us were in on it. Then he ranted and raved about how we were old enough to take responsibility for our actions and that he wanted the bill paid right away. Period. No begging. No pleading. No stalling." She hesitated. "I think he meant it."

"You don't think he'll call my parents, do you?" Joni asked. She was trying not to panic.

"Not if he gets the money," said Crystal.

"How long do we have?" Joni said. She felt as if she were a condemned prisoner asking about her death sentence.

"He gave us ten days," said Crystal. "I'm really sorry, Joni. If I hadn't seen that ad in the magazine..." She sounded close to tears.

"Hey, it's not your fault," Joni assured her. "We're all in this together. We should have started trying to get the money together before this."

After she hung up, Joni reviewed her options. There weren't very many. She had three dollars and seventy-two cents left from her allowance. Period.

Saving money was impossible with her measly allowance. And it was no use asking for money for her birthday. It was three months away. Worst of all, she didn't dare risk the wrath of her parents by asking for an advance. They were dead set against lending money, always saying she shouldn't get in the habit of running up debt. Besides, they'd probably ask why she needed the money. She couldn't risk that, either.

She eyed the telephone. There was one other option. The YMCA had a baby-sitting service. Kids who wanted to baby-sit had to take a class to learn about child care and first aid. If they passed, they could register to baby-sit. Parents could call the Y looking for a sitter and be matched up with someone who wanted to sit.

Joni had passed the class last year, but she hadn't taken a baby-sitting job since before school started. She'd been too busy with homework and her friends during the week and with Beau on weekends. But now, with just one weekend left before the phone bill was due, baby-sitting was the only choice she had.

With a deep sigh, she called the YMCA.

"YMCA, Mrs. Burnham speaking. May I help you?"

"Hi, Mrs. Burnham. This is Joni Sparkman. I'm calling to see if you have any baby-sitting jobs for this weekend."

"Boy, do we ever. I'm so glad you called," said Mrs. Burnham. "Friday or Saturday night?"

"Both," Joni said miserably.

"Okay. The Lattimores on Wavecrest need a sitter both nights for their three- and four-year-old boys. You've sat for them before, haven't you, Joni?"

"Yes," Joni replied, groaning inside.

Marky and Mikey Lattimore were holy terrors. But she had no choice. She had to do it. She thanked Mrs. Burnham and hung up.

She climbed into bed a little while later, feeling more depressed than she had in a long time. It had been one of the most terrible days of her life. But Saturday night would be even worse. While she was baby-sitting the Lattimore brats to pay off her phone bill, Megan and Beau would be having a great time together on their first date.

Chapter Thirteen

The next day, Thursday, Joni headed for school feeling even more depressed. In the Lindsey Jones mystery books, everything always turned out great by the end. Joni sighed. Her own detective work had led only to the beginning of an awesome disaster.

Crystal was waiting for her beside the front steps. Before Joni could ask where Su-Su was, their friend came running up waving a newspaper excitedly.

"Joni, did you read your horoscope this morning?"

Joni shook her head. She couldn't care less about her horoscope.

"Well, I did, and guess what it says?" said Su-Su.

"What?" Joni asked halfheartedly. Horoscopes bored her. It amazed her that someone as smart as

Su-Su actually believed they could predict the future.

"Listen to this. 'A situation that has caused many problems lately can be resolved if you are prepared to make fast decisions and major changes.' Isn't that awesome?" Su-Su said. "You're going to get Beau back."

Joni looked away. She didn't want either of her best friends to see the tears brimming in her eyes at the sound of Beau's name. It would take more than a horoscope to get him back now.

Joni turned back and gave Su-Su a skeptical look. "Get serious. I'm not going to hold my breath."

Su-Su snorted. "You know what your problem is, Joni Sparkman? Attitude. You've got to help these things along. Horoscopes really can work if you believe in them."

"I'm helping things along," Joni shot back. "Like paying my part of that phone bill we ran up. I called the Y last night and booked baby-sitting jobs for Friday *and* Saturday nights."

"You, too?" said Crystal. "I'm sitting from noon Saturday straight through to midnight. Yuck!"

"Well, I'm sitting, too," said Su-Su.

"I'm surprised your horoscope didn't tell you where to find a million dollars so you wouldn't have to," Joni said.

Su-Su flashed her a hurt look.

Instantly Joni regretted her words. "Gosh, Su-Su, I'm sorry," she said. "I didn't mean that. Honest. It's just that, well, things have been so rotten lately. But I shouldn't take it out on you."

Su-Su wound a long strand of red hair around her finger. "I know," she said softly. "This whole Beau thing has you really upset. I understand."

"We both do," said Crystal, her dimple showing. "Don't worry. We're going to stick by you and help you get through this. We promise."

Joni was on her way to gym class for third period when she heard a hoarse whisper behind her.

"Psst. Hey, over here!"

Puzzled, Joni looked around and did a double take. It was Beau. He was leaning out of an empty class-room and motioning for her to come inside.

Her stomach did a flip-flop. Beau wanted to see her!

She took a step toward him and stopped. *Oh, no,* she thought. *What if it wasn't me he was talking to?*

She glanced around quickly, but no one else in the crowded hallway was paying the slightest bit of attention. Beau was still looking in her direction.

"What do you want?" she demanded.

"Just come here," he insisted. "I need to talk to you."

A picture of the scene in the cafeteria yesterday flashed in Joni's mind. She could feel her anger returning. "I told you that I'm never speaking to you again," she snapped. "Remember?"

He shrugged and gave her a weak grin. "I know. Just talk to me for a minute. Okay?"

Joni sighed loudly so that he'd be sure to notice her exasperation. "What do you want?" she grumbled, walking toward him. "I have to get to gym class."

"I just thought you might like to know that my relatives aren't coming on Saturday after all." He hesitated, looking embarrassed. "I know you're baby-sitting Friday night, but we could do something Saturday night ... if you still want to."

Joni stared at him in disbelief. He sounded so sincere, and he was looking at her so hopefully. But he had been the boy in the second seat in the third row in the health room, and she had seen him flirting with Megan Scully with her very own eyes. Had he broken his date with Sneaking Around?

She shook her head and looked away. It was all so confusing. Beau had lied to her. Besides, did he expect her to swallow her pride and come racing back the moment he crooked his little finger?

"I can't," she said, raising her chin defiantly. "I'm baby-sitting Saturday night, too. And what about your date with Megan Scully?"

Beau shifted nervously from one foot to the other. "I don't have a date with Megan Scully, okay? She's just a friend."

Joni lowered her eyes and looked at the floor. Five minutes ago everything had seemed so clear. What did he mean, Megan was just a friend?

"Joni, I know you don't believe this, but I really do care about you. I know things look bad, but I just can't explain right now. Can't you get somebody else to sit for you Saturday night?"

Joni shook her head sadly. "No, I really can't. I need the money."

"What for?" Beau asked, sounding annoyed.

"I . . . I just do," she insisted. She couldn't tell him about Romance Rap. She would die of embarrassment if he ever found out. He would think she was silly. Or desperate. Even worse, he might make the connection between Romance Rap and Boy Talk.

"Hey, okay. If that's the way you feel," he said irritably. "I thought you liked me as much as I like you, but I guess I was wrong."

He stormed out of the empty classroom, leaving Joni standing there staring after him.

Now what have I done? she thought miserably. But deep down she knew. She had just given Beau an invitation to forget about her and start going out with his big pal Megan Scully.

Chapter Fourteen

"I can't *believe* you said that! Didn't you pay attention to *anything* your horoscope said?" Su-Su burst out when Joni told her and Crystal the latest about Beau.

It was almost three-thirty. The girls were at Crystal's house, getting ready to turn on the Boy Talk tape.

"In case you've forgotten, it said that something that had caused you problems could be fixed if you were willing to make big decisions and major changes, or something like that," said Su-Su. "But did you decide to change your baby-sitting schedule and give Beau another chance? Of course not." She slapped her forehead with the heel of her hand. "*You* don't believe in horoscopes."

Joni listened to Su-Su raging in silence. In a way Su-Su was right. She had done exactly the opposite of what her horoscope had said. But so what? Su-Su was right about something else, too. Joni didn't believe in horoscopes.

"I have to baby-sit," she told her friends, "There's no other way for me to get the money to pay Crystal's father unless I went to my parents. And"— she pulled a finger across her throat—"you know what that would mean."

"Hey, guys, it's show time," Crystal said. She glanced at her watch. She popped the Boy Talk tape into the answering machine and grinned. "Here goes. Let's see what we get today."

The telephone rang immediately.

Beep.

"Hi, Boy Talk. This is Likes a Stranger. I'm in seventh grade and I have a crush on a guy in eighth. My problem is, I don't know his name or anything about him. The only time I see him is in the halls. How can I get to know him?"

Crystal's face lit up. "Gosh, that's an easy one. She could smile and say hi every time she sees him, or she could start a conversation by asking him what time it is or telling him he looks like Keanu Reeves. There are a thousand things she could do."

"There you go again," said Su-Su, chuckling.

"Oh, Su-Su, will you disguise your voice again and

record my advice to Likes a Stranger?" Crystal asked.

"Sure," said Su-Su, then her face clouded. "Scratch that. April might call in to listen. I'd better not take a chance."

Before Crystal could respond the phone rang again.

Beep.

"It's me again," said a teary voice.

"That's Sneaking Around!" Joni shouted.

Crystal and Su-Su nodded, and the three of them gathered around the machine.

"You probably think I'm a pest by now, but I don't know who else to talk to," she began. "It's just that this morning in health class he broke our date. I asked him why, but he wouldn't tell me. I don't know if I did something to make him mad or if he's decided he likes the other girl best. I just want some advice on how to get him back. In case you don't recognize my voice, this is Sneaking Around."

Joni stared at the machine in astonishment. "He really did break his date with her," she said slowly.

Crystal's eyes lit up. "Oh, Joni, don't you think that means he still likes you, just like he said he does?"

"Exactly," said Su-Su, looking totally exasperated. "And if you had done what your horoscope said in the first place, like I told you, you'd have a date with him on Saturday night."

"Why don't you call Beau right now and tell him you've changed your mind and you'll go out with him after all?" suggested Crystal.

"I don't know how glad he'd be to hear from me," said Joni. "He was pretty mad when he walked away. Besides, I really do have to earn some money. If I cancel my Saturday-night job, I won't be able to pay your dad."

If only she didn't have to baby-sit, then maybe she would give Beau one more chance. Maybe he really could explain about Megan. Or maybe he'd just lie again. And then she would have made a fool of herself for believing him.

The ring of the telephone startled her.

Beep.

"This is Get Serious with a message for Sneaking Around. If you really want this guy, you'll have to fight for him. Besides, maybe he has a real reason for breaking your date. Maybe he has out-of-town relatives coming or something."

"Ha!" snorted Joni.

"Anyway," the caller jabbered on, "I think you should call him and act like everything is incredible between you. Then you can ask him to come over. I'm sure you'll know what to do when he gets there," she added with a giggle.

"Did you hear that!" demanded Joni, glaring at the answering machine. "Get Serious is telling Sneaking

Around to set a trap for *my* boyfriend!" Then she realized what she had just said. "My *ex*-boyfriend, that is," she corrected hastily.

"So what are you going to do?" asked Su-Su.

"I suppose you think I should read my horoscope for tomorrow," Joni said darkly. Then, feeling sheepish, she added, "Sorry. There I go again. But, guys, I *have* to baby-sit this weekend."

"Wait a minute," said Crystal. "I have a brilliant idea. You're supposed to sit Friday and Saturday nights, and I'm supposed to sit from noon Saturday until midnight. If we switched jobs, and I sat Friday and Saturday nights, and you did the marathon job on Saturday, you could go out with Beau on *Friday* night."

"That's awesome," said Su-Su. "Friday night is the night you and Beau usually go out anyway."

"And the hours we'd be sitting would be almost the same, so you wouldn't lose any money," Crystal added.

Joni gave her friends a huge smile as the idea sank in. "And if I'm lucky, I won't lose Beau either!" she said, jumping up and down. "Oh, Crystal! You're a genius! I'll call him as soon as I get home."

"Great. I'll go call the Y and tell them we want to switch," said Crystal. "Back in a sec!" she cried as she raced out of the room.

"Boy, I hope this works," said Joni. "I'd give anything if Get Serious had kept her mouth shut. All I need is Megan Scully chasing Beau while he's still mad at me."

"I can fix that!" Su-Su said. "I'll just erase Get Serious's message from the tape. That way Megan will never hear it!"

Joni watched as Su-Su carefully rewound the message tape to the beginning of the call from Get Serious, erased it and then set the tape to record again. Her heart felt as if it would burst with gratitude. "Thanks, Su-Su," she said. "You and Crystal are the best friends anyone could ever have."

Chapter Fifteen

All the way home from Crystal's house Joni worried about what she would say to Beau when she called him. *If she didn't lose her nerve.*

Hi, Beau. I'm not mad at you anymore over Megan Scully. Do you still want to do something this weekend?

Bogus, she thought. *He'd never fall for that. Maybe I should just say my baby-sitting job has been canceled and see what happens.*

But what if he turned her down? Or said he had another date with Megan? What would she do then?

When she got to her room she stared at the phone for a long time. *Maybe the best thing to do is just call him and see how the conversation goes,* she decided, and dialed his number.

Nobody answered.

She tried not to worry. Maybe Beau was at the Y shooting hoops with his friends. Or maybe he had gone over to Twister's house. Or Jason's. Or Parker's.

Or Megan's.

Su-Su had to have erased Get Serious's message before Megan could have heard it and done something stupid, like calling Beau and inviting him over.

Or had she?

Joni called Beau's number again. This time, to her relief, he answered.

"Maguire residence. This is Beau."

"Hi, Beau. Can you talk?"

"Yeah, I guess so," he replied halfheartedly.

A lump formed in Joni's throat. She had to push the words extra hard to make them come out.

"I don't have to baby-sit Friday night after all," she began, "and I was wondering if you'd still like to rent a movie and come over."

There was silence on the other end of the line.

"I thought you were mad," he said flatly.

"I was, but ..." Joni searched for words. She couldn't tell him that she knew for sure he had broken his date with Megan. "I guess I thought over what you said about really liking me. I wanted you to know that I like you, too."

All Joni could hear was the sound of her own heart beating. What was Beau thinking? Had she waited too long?

"Yeah, well, I could get a movie on my way over to your house," he said finally. "Unless … I mean … well, we could go out to the movie, the way we usually do," he added hurriedly.

Joni swallowed hard and gripped the receiver. He wanted to be seen with her in public again. He really *did* still like her!

"That would be great," she said, closing her eyes and collapsing on the bed.

After they hung up, Joni grinned up at the ceiling. She had done it! A million pounds seemed to have been lifted from her shoulders. She felt incredibly wonderful!

The next morning she took her time chosing what to wear to school. She wanted to look great when she saw Beau. She finally decided on her blue-and-white vintage dress and white ribbed tights. Beau had complimented her on that outfit once. Maybe seeing her in it would remind him of some of the good times they'd had.

Her hair was another matter. She had slept on it wrong, and little spikes stood straight out from the right side. No matter what she did to it, it looked as if it had gotten stuck in a blender.

And then there was her face. She inspected it closely and discovered that an ugly zit the size of the state of Texas had popped out on her forehead overnight.

She quickly plastered down her unruly hair with spray and hid the zit under a blob of her mother's makeup. Standing back, she surveyed herself in the mirror and felt a little better.

As soon as she got to school she started looking for Su-Su and Crystal. She found them outside the cafeteria, buying Danish from the vending machine.

"Hey, guys. Forget about food. I've got incredible news!" she said. The instant they turned around, she shot a fist into the air and cried, "I did it!"

"You mean you followed the advice in your horoscope?" Su-Su asked with a sly grin.

"As a matter of fact, I did," Joni retorted. "I called Beau after I got home from Boy Talk. First we were going to watch a movie at my house Friday night, but then he asked if I'd rather go out to a movie, the way we usually do. And I said yes. I think everything's okay between us again."

Joni knew she was grinning like an idiot. But she couldn't help it. She was so ecstatically happy!

Crystal clasped her hands in front of her chest. "Oh, Joni, that's wonderful! It's going to be so romantic. I wish I had a boyfriend like Beau," she added dreamily. "Especially if his name was Evan Byrnes."

"I wish I had a boyfriend, period," Su-Su said glumly. "I wouldn't care if his name was Evan or Beau or ... whoops! Speaking of whom ..."

She nodded toward the drinking fountain, where Beau and his three friends were squirting water at each other. They were ducking and jumping and laughing like crazy.

"Aren't you going to say something to him?" asked Crystal.

Joni tried to act casual as she watched Beau out of the corner of one eye. She wished he would stop horsing around long enough to notice her. She wanted him to see how nice she looked today. Maybe for once in his life he would compliment her in front of his friends. If he liked her as much as he said he did, he would.

"Let's walk past them," she said. "I want to see if he notices me."

They had taken only a few steps when Joni felt a spray of water hit her arm and splash onto her dress and face.

She gasped. "What—"

"I got her!" Twister yelled gleefully.

"Dan Turpin, you *jerk*! Look what you did! I'm soaked!" Joni cried, staring down at her dress. She had never been so furious in her life.

"Aw, poor Joni got all wet," Twister said, laughing loudly.

Beside him, Jason and Parker laughed too. Beau just stood there watching the whole scene.

Tears of rage filled Joni's eyes as she turned to

Beau. "Aren't you going to say anything?" she demanded. "That moron just squirted water all over me."

Beau looked uneasily from Joni to his friends and back to Joni again. Then he shrugged. "It's just water," he mumbled. "It's no big deal."

"*What?*" Joni cried. She couldn't believe how her so-called boyfriend was acting. She pulled at her skirt, which was sticking to her legs, and watched the water drip off the hem and gather in pools around her feet. "Just water? He did it on purpose. *That's* what the big deal is!"

"Come on, Joni, let's go," urged Crystal, pulling on Joni's arm.

"Yeah," said Su-Su. "These Neanderthals are too stupid to get the point."

Joni jerked away. "I'm not going anywhere until Dan apologizes," she said.

"Hang in there, Twister. Don't let her push you around," Jason called. "Right, Beau?"

This time Beau didn't hesitate. "Right," he said.

Joni stared at him in shock. It was happening again! Just when she thought Beau really cared about her, he started behaving like his obnoxious friends.

Without another word, she whirled around and stomped away.

Chapter Sixteen

Joni fumed all morning. She was furious at Twister for squirting her with water. But she was even more furious at Beau for siding with his friends. It didn't matter that her dress had dried quickly or that no one in her classes seemed to notice that it was wet. It was the principle of the thing.

On her way to the cafeteria, she spotted Beau ahead of her in the hall. He was leaning against the wall and watching her walk toward him. It was obvious that he was waiting for her.

Joni slowed down. Was he going to apologize again? she wondered. It was starting to seem as if he only apologized in private for all the stupid things he did in front of his friends.

If that's what he's planning, he can just forget it! Joni

thought angrily, and tried to rush past him.

Beau stepped in front of her. "Joni, hold up. I want to ask you something." He sounded more angry than apologetic.

"Go ahead," she snapped back, glaring up at him.

"Why do you have to have such an attitude about my friends?"

"What?" Joni screeched. "You've got to be kidding."

Beau's face darkened. "Oh, yeah? You know you're always trying to boss me around in front of the guys. How do you think that makes me feel? And they keep ragging on me and calling me a wimp for letting you run my life."

"I'm not bossing you around and I'm not trying to run your life," Joni replied, clutching her knapsack tightly. "I'm just trying to get you to stop acting so immature. We're supposed to be going out, in case you've forgotten. But when your dumb friends are around, you act just like them—like an obnoxious jerk!"

"Whoa!" said Beau, holding up his hands in protest. "I'm not immature, and don't you call my friends dumb, obnoxious jerks. So they like to kid around sometimes. So what? They don't hurt anybody, and they're a lot of fun to hang around with."

"You call *drenching* me fun?" Joni asked in disbelief. "And you just stood there, as if nothing had happened."

"They didn't drench you," Beau retorted. "They just got your dress a little wet. And then you went ballistic. What did you expect me to do? These guys are my friends. I've known them all my life. As far as I'm concerned, they're okay."

Joni stared at Beau. She was dumbfounded. And hurt. How could he defend those creeps and make it sound as if *she* were the one who was wrong?

"Well, if that's how you feel, maybe you'd better make a choice," she said. "Who is it going to be, them or me?"

Beau didn't answer.

Her heart beat furiously. All he had to do was remember all the seriously obnoxious things his friends had done just in the past few days. Then he would see what an easy choice it was.

"Well?" she pressed.

Beau shrugged. Then, looking sad, he turned and walked away.

Joni didn't hear much that went on in her afternoon classes. She had cried when she found Crystal and Su-Su in the crowded cafeteria and told them about Beau choosing his friends over her. She knew most of the kids at nearby tables were looking at her, but she didn't care.

"That only shows he's just as bad as they are," Su-Su had said loyally.

Crystal put her arm around Joni's shoulder and said sympathetically, "If he's going to act that way, you're better off without him."

Joni had protested at first, reminding her friends of how sweet Beau could be sometimes. How much fun they used to have together. And what a wonderful kisser he was. But the more she thought about it, the more she decided Crystal and Su-Su were right.

I don't want a boyfriend who cares more about his friends than about me, she thought sadly. *That's not what being boyfriend and girlfriend is all about. Megan can have him. And I'll use Boy Talk to tell her so.*

When the girls got to Crystal's house after school and were ready to start the Boy Talk tape, Joni turned to Crystal. "Is it okay if I use the phone in your room for a minute?"

"Sure," said Crystal.

Joni was glad her friend didn't ask why. She didn't want anyone trying to talk her out of what she was about to do.

She sat down on the edge of Crystal's bed and took a deep breath. Then she picked up the phone and punched in the number for Boy Talk.

Usually Joni giggled whenever she heard Su-Su's phony English accent, but today she was too depressed to laugh about anything. At the sound of the beep, she began to talk quickly.

"This is a message for Sneaking Around from His Ex. I just wanted you to know that today we broke up for good. I also wanted you to know that it wasn't your fault. So if he asks you out again, you don't need to feel guilty about going. It's okay with me."

Joni hung up and slumped back against the row of stuffed animals on Crystal's bed. Then she sat staring at nothing at all as a single tear rolled down her cheek.

Chapter Seventeen

The weekend came and went. Joni baby-sat and had four dollars left over after she paid off Mr. Britton. She was happy about that, but at the same time she couldn't keep her mind off Beau.

Had he bragged to his friends that he dumped her? The idea made prickles race up and down her back.

Did he go running to Sneaking Around? Did they go out together?

And what about Megan? Had she heard Joni's tape on Boy Talk?

Joni sighed sadly every time she thought about her own message on the hot line. *Boy Talk was supposed to help me with Beau*, she thought. *But it just made things worse.*

When she got to school Monday morning, she was

still feeling depressed. But as she started to open her locker, a folded piece of paper sticking out of a vent in the door caught her eye. A note!

Joni put her books down on the floor and pulled out the note. She held her breath as she opened it. Was it from Beau? Had he changed his mind about choosing his friends over her?

The instant she saw the handwriting, she knew the note wasn't from Beau. Then she looked at the bottom of the page and drew in her breath. It was from Megan Scully! Hurriedly, she read:

Dear Joni,

Thanks for leaving the message on Boy Talk. I just found out who you were a couple of days ago. I'm really sorry about what happened. I was thrilled when Beau asked me out, but I wasn't trying to break you two up. I didn't even know about you then. I felt awful when I found out. I just wanted you to know that.

Megan Scully

Joni leaned against her locker and read the note again.

Megan sounds like an awfully nice person, she thought. *I was wrong to blame her for my problems with Beau. I guess it's up to me to figure out what went wrong between us and whether our relationship is worth saving.*

She opened her locker and took out the books she needed for her morning classes. The first bell was about to ring.

Joni hurried down the hall and rounded a corner, almost smacking into Su-Su and Crystal.

"*There* you are!" Su-Su said breathlessly. "We were coming to find you."

"You'll never guess what April Mathis is saying now," said Crystal.

Joni's heart skipped a beat. "She knows?" she asked just above a whisper.

"You're going to love this," said Su-Su, grinning from ear to ear. Her eyes twinkled with mischief. "We just heard Molly Triola telling Brittany Preston that April says she's almost positive she knows who is behind Boy Talk. There's only one problem." She stopped, and her grin got even bigger.

"Well?" said Joni impatiently.

"The telephone number!" cried Su-Su. She hooked her thumbs around her red, white, and blue suspenders and did a little jig in the middle of the hall. "It's driving her crazy because she can't figure out whose it is!"

"Molly said she and April went to the beach yesterday," Crystal said excitedly, "and April took along a phone book and her student directory. She spent the entire afternoon looking up the phone numbers of every girl in school!"

Joni snickered. "Cool," she said. Then she gasped. "Oh, my gosh! What if April heard my message to Sneaking Around and recognized my voice?"

"Get serious, Joni," said Su-Su. "Leaving one message on Boy Talk is no proof that you're behind it. That'd make every single caller a suspect."

"I guess you're right," said Joni. "But if she suspects Su-Su of being the voice in the greeting, and she knows the three of us are best friends, she might put two and two together."

"We'll just have to be more careful," said Crystal.

"And what if Beau finds out I'm in on Boy Talk?" Joni wailed. "He'll think I'm a major busybody!"

"I thought you didn't like Beau anymore," said Crystal.

"I don't," Joni said. But deep down, she knew that wasn't true. She *did* still like Beau. A lot. And she really hoped things would work out between them.

How would Lindsey Jones solve this? she wondered.

All morning Joni racked her brain for a Lindsey Jones book with a similar plot. She thought about *The Case of the Missing Heiress* and *The Mystery in Skull Cove*, and her very favorite, *The Black Cat Clue*, but there was absolutely nothing in any of them that reminded her of her problem with Beau.

There was only one answer. She'd have to solve this one on her own.

Chapter Eighteen

When school was out for the day, the three girls pushed their way through the crowded halls and raced down the front steps of the building.

"Come on, guys, let's hurry," urged Su-Su. "I can't wait to see if April will call in today, now that she thinks she's such a genius."

"Maybe we shouldn't have Boy Talk today," said Joni. "It could be dangerous."

"Will you two shut up? Somebody's going to hear you talking about *you know what*," warned Crystal. She nodded toward a group of girls they had just passed on the sidewalk.

"You're right," said Su-Su. Then she stopped suddenly in her tracks. "Hey, check out who's straight ahead of us."

"Oh, no," muttered Joni.

Beau and his three jerky friends were huddled in the middle of the sidewalk, checking a pedal on Parker's bike. They'd have to pass right by them.

The closer Joni got, the louder her pulse pounded in her ears. She couldn't take her eyes off Beau. He looked so terrific. His blond hair glinted in the sunlight, and his tan was even darker than usual. She wanted desperately to call him aside. Maybe if they could just talk to each other...

But she couldn't do anything with his friends around. They would probably start teasing him again. That would make things worse than ever. Still, Joni thought wistfully, it wouldn't hurt to remind him she was alive.

Plastering a smile on her face, she called out, "Hi, Beau."

He glanced up from the bike and frowned. "Hi," he muttered and then looked down again.

Beside her, Su-Su sighed in exasperation. "Geez, Maguire, for the World's Best Kisser, you sure are a jerk." She slapped a hand over her mouth the instant the words were out and shot a glance at Joni.

Joni's heart stopped. She couldn't believe Su-Su had done this to her, even by mistake!

Beau snapped to attention. Anger gleamed in his eyes as he looked first at Su-Su and then at Joni.

Her knees turned to jelly. All she could do was

stare helplessly at Beau while his friends snickered behind him.

"The World's Best Kisser!" yelled Twister, doubling over with laughter. "Hey, everybody!" he called to kids passing by, "did you know that Beau Maguire is the world's best kisser?"

"Whoa, Schwartzy!" said Parker. "What's it like to be the world's best kisser?"

Then he and Jason began making loud smooching sounds.

Su-Su grabbed Joni's arm. "Oh, Joni, I'm sorry," she pleaded. "It just slipped out."

Joni was too horrified to look at her friend. All she could do was stare at Beau. If only she could erase the last few seconds.

Giving her a disgusted look, Beau pulled his bike off the grass and wheeled it toward the sidewalk.

Joni raced after him. She wanted to offer some kind of explanation, but the words stuck in her throat.

"How did she find out about that?" he demanded when he looked around and saw her.

Joni could feel her face turning red. "I guess I must have told her," she confessed.

Anger flashed in his eyes again. "How could you tell them a thing like that? It was private. You know, just between us."

"They're my *friends*," Joni insisted. "I tell them everything."

Beau's brows rose. "Even about us?"

Joni nodded miserably. She knew what he was probably thinking, but he just didn't understand. "They're my best friends."

"Well, I have friends, too," said Beau. "Remember? You complain about them all the time. And you try to boss me around in front of them."

"I do not!" said Joni. "When have I ever bossed you around in front of your friends?"

"How about when I got invited to April's party and you didn't? Remember that?" he demanded. "They're still on my case about that one."

Joni glared at him in silence. *So I was a little bossy one time,* she thought. *Big deal.*

"But at least I don't tell the guys private stuff about us. How can you tell me to forget about what *my* friends say when you obviously blab everything to yours?"

Joni was dumbfounded. She struggled to find words as he pushed his bike away from her.

"Beau, wait!" she called.

Beau stopped, but he didn't turn around.

Joni took a deep breath. "At least I didn't cheat on you," she blurted.

It seemed like forever before Beau lowered the kick stand on his bike and turned to face her.

"You've got to understand," he began, fumbling over the words. "Those guys have been my friends for a long time. And sometimes I do things I don't even want to do to get them off my case."

"Like what?" Joni snapped.

He shifted his weight from one foot to the other. "Just stuff. Like ... you know."

Joni folded her arms. "Like asking out another girl?" she said. "Is that why you wanted to date Megan Scully? To get your friends off your back about me?"

He nodded. "I told Megan not to tell anybody, and I was just going over to her house to watch TV. I didn't think you'd find out."

Joni could hardly believe she was hearing right. How could a nice guy like Beau Maguire do something so stupid just to look good in front of his friends?

I'll never understand boys, she thought. *And what would Sneaking Around think if she knew the truth?*

"Poor Megan," said Joni aloud, shaking her head. "You used her, and now she has a humongous crush on you. How could you do a thing like that?"

Beau sighed in frustration. "I told you. The guys were giving me a hard time about you. Besides, I didn't know she liked me that much. Not at first, anyway. We talked sometimes in health class. We were just friends. Then that night at April's party, Twister and Hatchet Man were really giving me grief about being there without you and how mad you were going to be. Stuff like that."

He hesitated before going on. "Anyway, I'd been talking to Megan earlier, and the idea just popped into my head. I decided to find her again and ask her out in front of my friends. When they saw me do that, they'd stop teasing me about you. I thought I could go over to her house for a while on Friday and just talk, the way we always did in class. It'd be real easy, and I'd be off the hook with the guys. I know it sounds pretty dumb now, but it made sense at the time."

"And you thought I'd never find out," Joni murmured.

"Yeah. How *did* you, anyway?" asked Beau.

Joni gulped. She could never tell him about Boy Talk. Not in a million years!

"Oh ..." she began and shrugged helplessly. "I just ... heard it ... somewhere."

When she looked back at Beau, he was staring off in space. All of their friends had disappeared by now, and the sidewalk was deserted.

Joni thought back over their conversation. Then she said slowly, "I guess I didn't realize how important your buddies are to you, Beau. I mean, guys are always goofing around and acting stupid. It never seems as if they take things that seriously."

"Believe me, we do," Beau said. "But we're different from girls. There are some things we don't talk to each other about."

This was it. The big moment when she and Beau might be able to make up. But for that to happen, Joni knew she would have to admit that she had been as wrong as he had. It was true she shouldn't have told her friends super-private things. But he had hurt her. Badly. Would making up with him be worth it?

She gazed silently at Beau, remembering all the great times they'd shared. Especially the night she'd told him he was the World's Best Kisser.

She hesitated another instant and then took a deep breath. "Maybe I should tape my mouth shut when I'm around Su-Su and Crystal," she said.

Beau grinned sheepishly. She could definitely see relief in his eyes. "Maybe I should punch out anybody who teases me about you."

"And maybe I'll *also* tape my mouth shut when I'm around your friends," Joni said, starting to laugh.

"And maybe *I* won't pay so much attention to their dumb opinions," said Beau. He pushed up the kick stand and nodded toward his bike. "Come on. I'll ride you home."

"Thanks," Joni murmured. She jumped on the back of the bike, her heart bursting with happiness. Everything was going to be okay!

Chapter Nineteen

When Beau dropped Joni off at her house a few minutes later, they made plans to go to a movie on Friday night.

"I'm really glad we straightened things out," Beau said.

"Me, too," said Joni.

He leaned across the handlebars, and Joni was sure he was going to kiss her. But just then a carload of older kids went by, windows down and music blasting.

Joni wasn't sure if she heard one of them yell something or not, but Beau jerked upright and gave her a sheepish grin.

"Guess I'd better go," he said.

She watched until he was out of sight. Then she turned around and hurried straight to Crystal's.

"Here I am, guys, and guess *what?*" she shouted when she burst into Mr. Britton's office. Su-Su and Crystal were sitting around the answering machine.

Joni didn't wait for her friends to reply. "We're back together!"

"Incredible!" said Crystal, shaking her head.

"Then he's not still mad about what I said?" Su-Su asked hopefully.

"Well, he's not really happy about it," Joni admitted, "but it's not your fault. I told you guys something I should have kept private. Beau and I talked things over. I think we understand each other a lot better now."

"What about Megan? Did he explain about *her?*" Su-Su asked.

"Yeah, but promise you won't—whoops!" said Joni. She clamped a hand over her mouth and giggled. "Sorry, guys. What he told me was private. I hope you'll understand, but I'm going to keep my mouth shut about some things from now on."

"Rats!" said Su-Su, grinning.

"Come on, Joni. We're your best friends," pleaded Crystal.

"Nope. A promise is a promise." Joni sat down beside her. "But wait until you hear the idea I've got about April. I've been thinking about how she wants to find out who's running Boy Talk."

"Right," said Crystal. "It's making me *real* nervous."

"Me, too," said Su-Su. "She could bust up Boy Talk just as it's really getting going."

A big grin spread over Joni's face. "Want to hear something seriously brilliant?"

"Yes!" Su-Su and Crystal shouted in unison.

They huddled around the desk as Joni told them her plan. When she had finished, she looked at Su-Su and asked, "Do you think you can do it?"

"You bet I can," said Su-Su gleefully. "Let's get to work on the script."

Five minutes later, Su-Su headed for Crystal's room to call Boy Talk.

Beep.

"Hi, Boy Talk. This is April Mathis," said a voice that sounded almost exactly like April's. "I've been telling everybody that I know for sure who's behind Boy Talk. Well, here's a hint. She has violet eyes and shoulder-length brown hair and is captain of the cheerleading squad. Do you think you can figure out who she is?"

Su-Su burst back into the room a moment later. "How was my imitation?" she asked eagerly.

"It was perfect," said Crystal, her dimple deepening. "April will go absolutely crazy."

"It will be all over school tomorrow that April's behind Boy Talk," said Joni. "She'll have a lot of explaining to do."

"And she won't have time to cause us trouble," put in Su-Su.

"But she won't give up," Joni pointed out. "This may buy us a little more time, but we'll have to think of a way to throw her off track for good."

She felt a tingle run up her spine. Things were just about perfect now. Boy Talk was a huge success. April Mathis hadn't found out who was running it. And best of all, she and Beau were back together.

Take that, Lindsey Jones, Joni thought. She smiled to herself just as the telephone rang again.

Hi, guys! This is Joni. Hope you enjoyed Sneaking Around. *Here's a sneak peek at Book #2:* Dude in Distress:

"I know I'll never get over Alison," Evan said. "There's no way."

"Of course you will," Crystal said quickly. "I mean, it might take some time, but you'll find someone else. There are tons of terrific girls in the world."

"Yeah?" Evan scoffed. "Like who?"

Crystal swallowed hard. She wanted to shout, "Like me!" But the words stuck in her throat.

"See?" Evan said triumphantly. "You can't think of anyone. There'll never be another girl like Alison. It's not just that she's pretty. Her personality is special, too. I've never met anyone like her before."

Crystal walked along in silence, her heart breaking all over again.

When they reached the school grounds, Evan stopped and turned toward her. "Hey, Crys, thanks for listening. I guess I needed to talk more than I thought. You're a real buddy." Then he chucked her gently under the chin and loped off toward his friends.

BETSY HAYNES wrote her first book when she was nine years old. It was about a frog named Peppy who leaves his lily pad to see the world. Today most of her books are based upon things that happened to her and her friends when they were in middle school and junior high—Betsy says she's forever thirteen!

Betsy lives on Marco Island, Florida. She and her husband, Jim have two grown children, two dogs, and a black cat with extra toes. She enjoys traveling and spending time on her boat, *Nut & Honey*. And she really loves to talk on the phone!

WRITE TO "DEAR BOY TALK"

NEED ADVICE ABOUT

DATING?   **FRIENDSHIP?**   **ROMANCE?**

Joni, Crystal, and Su-Su may have an answer for you!

Just write to *Dear Boy Talk* at this address:

Random House, Inc.
201 East 50th Street
New York, NY 10022

Attn: "Dear Boy Talk"
28th Floor

Let us know what's on your mind. From secret crushes to broken hearts to major embarrassments, Boy Talk™ can help! We can't publish every letter, but we can promise to print a select few in the back of every new Boy Talk book.

Too shy to share your romance problems? Boy Talk fans can give advice for readers' problems, too! Letters will begin appearing in Boy Talk #2: DUDE IN DISTRESS. Just pick a problem and write to the above address— and you just might see *your* letter in print!

And here's the best part: Everybody who writes to Dear Boy Talk will get—**absolutely free!**—

📞 a Boy Talk™ address book that doubles as a key chain

and

📞 a prepaid calling card good for five free minutes of phone time to any number in the U.S.*

So don't put your romance on hold—
write to Dear Boy Talk today!